GW01191669

J.T.'s LADIES RIDE AGAIN

J.T.'s ladies prove once again that they are more than a match for any man in the tough and dangerous West. Woman Deputy Alice Fayde copes with three murderous criminals; Amanda 'Blonde Genius' Tweedle saves the daughters of gentlefolk from blackmail; Rita Yarborough finds herself in deadly danger when she gets involved in a race-track scam; and Belle Starr, the lady outlaw, proves that she can beat a gang of card-sharps at their own game—but is very glad of the help of Calamity Jane!

And when faced with the direst peril, none of these gallant ladies ever needs a 'hero' to rescue her!

Ole Devil Hardin series

YOUNG OLE DEVIL
OLE DEVIL AND THE CAPLOCKS
OLE DEVIL AND THE MULE TRAIN
OLE DEVIL AT SAN JACINTO
GET URREA

The Civil War series

COMANCHE
YOU'RE IN COMMAND NOW, MR. FOG
THE BIG GUN
UNDER THE STARS AND BARS
THE FASTEST GUN IN TEXAS
A MATTER OF HONOUR
KILL DUSTY FOG!
THE DEVIL GUN
THE COLT AND THE SABRE
THE REBEL SPY
THE BLOODY BORDER
BACK TO THE BLOODY BORDER

The Floating Outfit series

THE YSABEL KID
.44 CALIBRE MAN
A HORSE CALLED MOGOLLON
GOODNIGHT'S DREAM
FROM HIDE AND HORN
SET TEXAS BACK ON HER FEET
THE HIDE AND TALLOW MEN
THE HOODED RIDERS
QUIET TOWN
TRAIL BOSS
WAGONS TO BACKSIGHT
TROUBLED RANGE
SIDEWINDER
RANGELAND HERCULES
McGRAW'S INHERITANCE
THE HALF BREED
WHITE INDIANS
THE WILDCATS
THE BAD BUNCH
THE FAST GUN
CUCHILO
A TOWN CALLED YELLOWDOG
TRIGGER FAST
THE MAKING OF A LAWMAN
THE TROUBLE BUSTERS
THE GENTLE GIANT
DECISION FOR DUSTY FOG

DIAMONDS, EMERALDS, CARDS AND COLTS
THE CODE OF DUSTY FOG
SET A-FOOT
THE LAW OF THE GUN
THE PEACEMAKERS
TO ARMS! TO ARMS! IN DIXIE!
HELL IN THE PALO DURO
GO BACK TO HELL
THE SOUTH WILL RISE AGAIN
THE QUEST FOR BOWIE'S BLADE
BEGUINAGE
BEGUINAGE IS DEAD!
MASTER OF TRIGGERNOMETRY
THE RUSHERS
BUFFALO ARE COMING!
THE FORTUNE HUNTERS
RIO GUNS
GUN WIZARD
THE TEXAN
OLD MOCCASINS ON THE TRAIL
THE RIO HONDO KID
OLE DEVIL'S HANDS AND FEET
WACO'S DEBT
THE HARD RIDERS
THE FLOATING OUTFIT
APACHE RAMPAGE
THE RIO HONDO WAR
THE MAN FROM TEXAS
GUNSMOKE THUNDER
THE SMALL TEXAN
THE TOWN TAMERS
RETURN TO BACKSIGHT
TERROR VALLEY
GUNS IN THE NIGHT

Waco series

WACO'S BADGE
SAGEBRUSH SLEUTH
ARIZONA RANGER
WACO RIDES IN
THE DRIFTER
DOC LEROY, M.D.
HOUND DOG MAN

Calamity Jane series

CALAMITY, MARK AND BELLE
COLD DECK, HOT LEAD
THE BULL WHIP BREED
TROUBLE TRAIL

THE COW THIEVES
THE HIDE AND HORN SALOON
CUT ONE, THEY ALL BLEED
CALAMITY SPELLS TROUBLE
WHITE STALLION, RED MARE
THE REMITTANCE KID
THE WHIP AND THE WAR LANCE
THE BIG HUNT

Waxahachie Smith series

NO FINGER ON THE TRIGGER
SLIP GUN
CURE THE TEXAS FEVER

Alvin Dustine 'Cap' Fog series

YOU'RE A TEXAS RANGER, ALVIN FOG
RAPIDO CLINT
THE JUSTICE OF COMPANY 'Z'
'CAP' FOG, TEXAS RANGER, MEET MR. J.G. REEDER
THE RETURN OF RAPIDO CLINT AND MR. J.G. REEDER

The Rockabye County series

THE SIXTEEN DOLLAR SHOOTER
THE LAWMEN OF ROCKABYE COUNTY
THE SHERIFF OF ROCKABYE COUNTY
THE PROFESSIONAL KILLERS
THE 1/4 SECOND DRAW
THE DEPUTIES
POINT OF CONTACT
THE OWLHOOT
RUN FOR THE BORDER
BAD HOMBRE

Bunduki series

BUNDUKI
BUNDUKI AND DAWN
SACRIFICE FOR THE QUAGGA GOD
FEARLESS MASTER OF THE JUNGLE

Miscellaneous titles

J.T.'s HUNDREDTH
J.T.'s LADIES
IS-A-MAN
WANTED! BELLE STARR
MORE J.T.'s LADIES
SLAUGHTER'S WAY
TWO MILES TO THE BORDER
BLONDE GENIUS (**Written in collaboration with Peter Clawson**)

J.T.'s LADIES RIDE AGAIN

J.T. Edson

ROBERT HALE • LONDON

This edition 1991

ISBN 0 7090 4324 4

Robert Hale Limited
Clerkenwell House
Clerkenwell Green
London EC1R 0HT

Printed and Bound in Great Britain by WBC Print Ltd., and WBC Bookbinders Ltd., Bridgend, Mid Glamorgan.

To the memory of all the idiots of the press who have written articles about me entitled things like, 'The Fastest Pen In Melton Mowbray' and filled with the most stupid, snob-orientated pseudo-'cowboy' jargon never to be seen on the pages of mine or anybody else's Western books. May the blue bird of happiness fly over them—when it has dysentery, because that is catching.

Contents

Author's Note

When supplying us with the information from which we produce our books, one of the strictest rules imposed upon us by the present day members of what we call the 'Hardin, Fog and Blaze' clan and the 'Counter' family is that we *never* under any circumstances disclose their true identities, nor their present locations. Therefore, we are instructed to *always* employ sufficient inconsistencies to ensure neither can happen.

To save our 'old hands' repetition, but for the benefit of new readers, we have given information regarding family backgrounds and special qualifications of Woman Deputy Alice Fayde, Rita Yarborough and Calamity Jane in the form of Appendices.

We realize that, in our present 'permissive' society, we could use the actual profanities employed by various people in the narrative. However, we do not concede a spurious desire to create 'realism' is any excuse to do so.

Lastly, as we refuse to pander to the current 'trendy' usage of the metric system, except when referring to the calibre of certain firearms traditionally measured in millimetres—i.e. Walther P-38, 9mm—we will continue to employ miles, yards, feet, inches, stones, pounds and ounces, when quoting distances or weights.

J.T. EDSON,
Active Member, Western Writers of America,
MELTON MOWBRAY,
Leicestershire,
England.

INTRODUCTION

Having been an avid reader of the wonderful action-escapism-adventure fiction which had its vintage years from the mid-1930s to mid-1950s, I could not help noticing how small a part was allocated to what my generation could still refer to respectfully as the 'gentle sex' without provoking screams of 'male chauvinist pig' from over-reacting supporters of 'Women's Lib'. In fact, with *very* few exceptions all through that period,[1] action-escapism-adventure fiction in books, movies and, later, television series, tended to be very much a masculine

1. Doctor Clark 'Doc' Savage, Jr. and Richard 'the Avenger' Benson – no connection with the British television series of that name – whose biographies were recorded in a considerable number of volumes apiece by Kenneth Robeson,[1a] had respectively Patricia Savage and Nellie Grey among their coterie of regular 'sidekicks'. However, competent as each lady undoubtedly was in other fields, including unarmed combat, neither was ever called upon to quell a villainess. In fact, their main function appeared to be falling into dire peril from which Doc or the Avenger, depending upon the series, was obliged to rescue them.

1a. It is rumoured 'Kenneth Robeson' was actually the 'house name' for several writers and the most prolific of them was Lester Dent.

domain.[2] Heroines were expected to be beautiful, shapely and virtuous – this being in the days before sexual promiscuity was turned by the media into an apparently desirable and essential trait upon which, rather than any worthwhile endeavour, one's success or failure in life is judged[3] – but meek, mild and completely dependent upon the hero for protection whenever danger threatened.

Therefore, on embarking upon my career as a writer, I decided to try to remedy the situation.[4] My heroines would be beautiful, shapely, and almost always virtuous. However, they would not be dependent upon *anybody* except themselves when in a perilous situation.

Martha, 'Calamity Jane' Canary was the first of my 'ladies' to be given a full 'starring' role and, so far, is the only one to having attained the status of having a series of

2. *Although only rarely used in a similar capacity in television series of any* genre, *ladies fared better than in books from action-escapism-adventure movies, which attracted people to the cinema in vast numbers before Hollywood's 'message' and 'socially significant' film phase drove them away. As I pointed out in the Introduction to Calamity Jane's section of* J.T.'S HUNDREDTH, *they were especially useful in Western films for dealing with a villainess, as her sex precluded the hero from being able to handle her physically as he did her male associates.*

3. *Ever since I saw two little mongrel dogs 'having it off' in the gutter outside my 'spiritual' home, the Half Moon Public House, in Melton Mowbray, I have realized that sex – as it has been exploited since the commencement of the 'permissive society' in the early 1960s – is just an ego trip for non-entities. Requiring no training, manual dexterity, nor great effort to attain, as both sexes have become so brain-washed into believing it is the most important thing in the world, it is ideal for that purpose.*

4. *How I embarked upon my career as a writer is explained in the main* Introduction *to:* J.T.'S HUNDREDTH.

her own.[5] However, the lady outlaw, Belle Starr, preceded her in print by making a 'guest' appearance in my second published work, Part Four, 'A Lady Known As Belle', THE HARD RIDERS.[6] She also made a 'guest' appearance in, Case One, 'The Set-Up', SAGEBRUSH SLEUTH – which was later converted to a 'starring' role in its 'expansion', WACO'S BADGE – and paved the way for Calamity's appearance in print by there being a reference to a scar on her hand which was acquired when they fought one another on their first meeting in, Part One, 'The Bounty On Belle Starr's Scalp, TROUBLED RANGE and its 'expansion', CALAMITY, MARK AND BELLE.[7]

Due to new information I received from Alvin Dustine 'Cap' Fog allowing me to produce, WHITE INDIANS, an

5. *Information about the family background and special qualifications of Calamity Jane are given in:* APPENDIX THREE.

6. *The full story of this incident is recorded in an 'expansion':* JESSE JAMES'S LOOT.

7. *Belle Starr makes 'guest' appearances in:* RANGELAND HERCULES; THE BAD BUNCH; DIAMONDS, EMERALDS, CARDS AND COLTS; THE CODE OF DUSTY FOG; THE GENTLE GIANT; HELL IN THE PALO DURO; GO BACK TO HELL; THE QUEST FOR BOWIE'S BLADE; Part Two, 'We Hang Horse Thieves High', J.T.'S HUNDREDTH; *and her death is reported in;* GUNS IN THE NIGHT.

7a. *The lady outlaw also 'stars' – no pun intended – in:* WANTED! BELLE STARR.

7b. *I have occasionally been asked why the 'Belle Starr' I describe differs so greatly from a photograph which appears in numerous books. The researches of the world's foremost fictionist geanologist, Philip José Farmer – author of, amongst other works,* TARZAN ALIVE, A Definitive Biography Of Lord Greystoke *and* DOC SAVAGE, His Apocalyptic Life – *have established the 'Belle Starr' for whom I have the honour to be biographer is not the same person as another equally famous bearer of the name and whose picture it is. However, 'Cap' Fog and Andrew Mark 'Big Andy' Counter have asked that Mr Farmer and I keep her true identity a secret and we intend to do so.*

'expansion' of, Part One, 'The Half Breed', THE HALF BREED, Annie 'Is-A-Man' Singing Bear was introduced and she made a 'guest' appearance in, BUFFALO ARE COMING. She had also 'starred' in IS-A-MAN – explaining how she became accepted as a Comanche warrior and gained her 'man-name' – and in Part One, 'To Separate Innocence From Guilt', MORE J.T.'s LADIES.

In response to my suggestion, 'Cap' Fog's wife, 'Miz Rita', née Yarborough, put pressure to bear upon him to include her adventures when he authorized me to chronicle the history of Company 'Z', Texas Rangers, in the *Alvin Dustine 'Cap' Fog* series. Despite being proud of and willing to give full credit for the excellence of her participation, he admitted his reluctance in the first place was due to her having been compelled to behave in a less than lady-like fashion on more than one occasion.[8]

With the exception of THE SIXTEEN DOLLAR SHOOTER – placed first in the chronological listing of the *Rockabye County* series, although written later than most of the other entries – Woman Deputy Alice Fayde has had full 'starring' status since the original title, THE PROFESSIONAL KILLERS, ushered herself, her partner, Deputy Sheriff Bradford 'Brad' Counter, and the other members of the Rockabye County Sheriff's Office on to the printed page in 1986.[9] She is, in fact, the senior member of their investigative team and is involved in a far greater share of the physical action than any other female peace officer with whom I have come

8. Rita Yarborough participates actively in: RAPIDO CLINT; Part Two, 'Behind A Locked And Bolted Door', MORE J.T.'S LADIES; THE JUSTICE OF COMPANY 'Z' *and* THE RETURN OF RAPIDO CLINT AND MR. J.G. REEDER.

9. My series of short stories entitled, THE SHERIFF OF ROCKABYE COUNTY, *was published in* VICTOR, *a boys paper, during 1965. However, Woman Deputy Alice Fayde is not in it and, although Sheriff Jack Tragg appeared under his right name, Deputy Sheriff Bradford 'Brad' Counter became 'Mike Counter' for some reason which was never explained.*

into contact via books, movies, or television 'police' series.

I have covered the background for the creation of the *Bunduki* series in my introduction to that section of J.T.'S HUNDREDTH and there is no point in repeating it in full. However, although I regard Edgar Rice Burroughs as the greatest action-escapism-adventure writer of all time, I confess I have always considered he never exploited any of his heroines to their full potential. This was especially true of Jane, wife of Tarzan of the Apes. Except in TARZAN'S QUEST, when she made a bow and arrow so she could hunt to help feed herself and some friends stranded in the jungle by a plane crash, she rarely demonstrated whatever survival techniques she must have learned from her husband. On being granted permission by Edgar Rice Burroughs, Inc., to introduce Dawn Drummond-Clayton and James Allenvale 'Bunduki' Gunn, respectively adoptive great-granddaughter and adopted son of Lord and Lady Greystoke, I followed my usual practice of allowing her to be as completely self reliant as all my other 'ladies'. I reasoned that, having had such a family background, she would have had training which would allow her to cope without needing to scream for help the moment any danger threatened even though – particularly in every 'Tarzan' movie I have seen[10] – this appeared to be all Jane was capable of doing.

Although not all of them appear in this volume, for reasons of space rather than because they are less physic-

10. In the 1950 movie, TARZAN AND THE SLAVE GIRL, *'Jane' (Vanessa Brown) demonstrated some skill at unarmed combat by defeating the considerably larger 'slave girl', 'Lola', (Denise Darcel) in a brief tussle, but reverted to type on being captured by the slave traders and did nothing more positive than wait to be rescued by 'Tarzan' (Lex Barker).*

ally active and competent: Bell 'the Rebel Spy' Boyd;[11] 'Miz Freddie' Fog, née Lady Winifred Amelia Besgrove-Woodstole – although she mostly appeared under the alias, 'Freddie Woods'[12]; Elizabeth 'Betty' Hardin[13];

11. Information about the family background and special qualifications of Belle 'the Rebel Spy' Boyd is given in various volumes of the Civil War *and* Floating Outfit *series.*

11a. An excellent illustration of Belle Boyd was produced to share the cover art for THE WHIP AND THE WAR LANCE *with Calamity Jane. Regrettably, she was changed for the masculine figure which appeared on the finished product because the sales supervisor of a major book distributor informed Transworld Publishers – as the company was then – a 'cowboy' book had to have a 'cowboy' on the cover, presumably because he thought the readers of Westerns could not identity it as such without that aid. In my opinion, the attitude represents the typical middle class-middle management snob mentality where the action-escapism-adventure side of Western* genre *is concerned.*

12. Mrs Winifred Amelia Fog appears as 'Freddie Woods' in: THE MAKING OF A LAWMAN; THE TROUBLE BUSTERS; DECISION FOR DUSTY FOG *(which explains why she was living under an alias in the United States);* DIAMONDS, EMERALDS, CARDS AND COLTS; THE CODE OF DUSTY FOG; THE GENTLE GIANT; THE FORTUNE HUNTERS; WHITE STALLION, RED MARE; THE WHIP AND THE WAR LANCE, *and* Part Five, 'The Butcher's Fiery End', J.T.'S LADIES. *She also makes a 'guest' appearance under her married name in:* NO FINGER ON THE TRIGGER.

13. Elizabeth 'Betty' Hardin appears in: Part Five, 'A Time For Improvisation, Mr Blaze', J.T.'S HUNDREDTH; Part Four, 'It's Our Turn To Improvise, Miss Blaze', J.T.'S LADIES; KILL DUSTY FOG!; THE BAD BUNCH; McGRAW'S INHERITANCE; Part Two, 'The Quartet', THE HALF BREED, *its 'expansion',* HOLD FOR RANSOM; MASTER OF TRIGGERNOMETRY; THE RIO HONDO WAR *and* GUNSMOKE THUNDER.

13a. 'Cap' Fog refuses to make any statement upon the exact relationship between Betty and her 'grandfather', General Jackson Baines 'Ole Devil' Hardin, C.S.A.

Amanda 'the School Swot' Tweedle[14] and two generations of Miss Amelia Penelope Diana 'Benkers' Benkinsop[15], have all played their part in proving 'ladies' are fully capable of holding their own in action-escapism-adventure literature.

However, enough of explanations!

Now...

J.T.'S LADIES RIDE AGAIN

14. Amanda 'the School Swot' Tweedle appears in: BLONDE GENIUS *and* Part One, 'Fifteen The Hard Way', J.T.'S LADIES.

15. Some activities of the very competent British lady criminal, Amelia Penelope Diana 'Benkers' Benkinsop, during her visit to the United States in the mid-1870s are recorded in: BEGUINAGE IS DEAD!; Part Three, 'Birds Of A Feather', WANTED! BELLE STARR *and* Part Five, 'The Butcher's Fiery End', J.T.'S LADIES.

15a. Information about a descendant of the above 'Benkers' – who also followed the family tradition of retaining the full name regardless of who the father might be – Miss Amelia Penelope Diana Benkinsop, G.C., M.A., B.Sc. (Oxon), owner of Benkinsop's Academy For The Daughters Of Gentlefolk in England, is given in the two titles 'starring' Amanda Tweedle.

PART ONE

WOMAN DEPUTY ALICE FAYDE
In
ALL DONE WITHOUT DEDUCTIVE REASONING

CHAPTER ONE

Lounging against the side of the Ford sedan, the door of which he had found was unlocked thus allowing him to start the engine, Manuel Santoval was successful in conveying the impression of doing nothing more than waiting for somebody to join him. Nevertheless, his purpose was far from being so harmless and innocent. He and his brothers, Otón and Rafael, were engaged upon their usual business of stealing cars from the parking lots of shopping malls. Since graduating from petty larceny to the more lucrative form of crime, they had established a procedure – termed a m.o., *modus operandi*, by law enforcement agencies – which had so far proved satisfactory and successful.

When carrying out the thefts, the brothers always selected three newish vehicles in the medium price range as these found a ready market from dishonest second-hand car salesmen or from the owners of 'body shops' for stripping down and being sold as 'spare parts'. They had never attached themselves to any organized ring of car thieves and regularly changed their venue from town to town across Texas. By doing so, they had avoided arrest for their main illicit activities and also for the potentially more serious sideline which occasionally added to their profits.

Keeping watch while Otón and Rafael were making the chosen cars ready to drive away, Manuel decided an opportunity was being presented for him to put the second of their illicit activities into effect. Looking over the magazine he was pretending to read, he studied with a calculating and predatory gaze the woman who had parked a powder blue Cadillac coupe of the latest model and was walking along an alley left between other vehicles towards the east side entrance to the Leander Shopping Mall. Regarding himself as an authority on the opposite sex, particularly where deciding upon their potential as victims for mugging was concerned, he drew certain satisfying conclusions from his study. Therefore, although he and his brothers would not have considered her car suitable for their purposes, he concluded that she could provide a useful addition to the bankroll they were collecting to tide them over during the extended visit which recent events required they paid to Mexico.

Five foot seven in height, the whole appearance of the woman was indicative of wealth and good living. Her mass of frizzy blonde hair had cost a great deal of money to achieve such a casual-seeming style. While she was not ravishingly beautiful her face, adorned by sunglasses with enormous rhinestone decorated rims was attractive. However, it was so heavily made up, he suspected she was trying to mask traces of her age. Confirmation was suggested by a wide green silk scarf around her throat. Such was frequently used to cover an area of the female anatomy less susceptible than the features to treatment intended to remove the ravages of time. A massive Navajo silver and turquoise necklace hung around her neck. There were matching wide bracelets on her wrists, but any rings she might have worn were concealed beneath white gloves. Cut with an elegance indicative of having been obtained from some exclusive shop in Upton Heights, a loose fitting white blouse and baggy-legged green slacks tucked into calf high black boots could not entirely conceal she had a very good figure.

Despite possessing a lecherous disposition, at that moment, Manuel was more interested in the woman's jewellery and the bulky bag in her right hand than in her physical attractions. He was satisfied the adornments were of genuine Indian manufacture and very valuable. Furthermore, in addition to whatever money was in the latter, there was sure to be several credit cards and these could be sold to a local fence who he had been told specialised in such items.

Natural caution rather than the expectation of intervention by other people caused Manuel to decide how he should act. As far as he could detect, nobody was close in the big parking lot who might intervene. The scrutiny he had carried out on arriving with his brothers had established there were only stationary and, to all appearances, unoccupied vehicles in the vicinity. Nevertheless, any screams she made before he was able to silence her, might be heard and bring help from the armed security guards employed by the shopping mall. Or, as had happened a short while earlier in San Antonio, somebody might come into sight and raise the alarm. Experience elsewhere had taught him that it was advisable to go for the more readily acquired property first. The jewellery was worth stealing, but its removal could not be effected with the same speed needed to snatch the handbag. Should there be a need to escape before he could acquire the jewellery, he would have the bag in his grasp ready to take away. On the other hand, if an immediate departure was not called for, it could be used as an extemporized club to stun her while he removed the necklace and bracelets.

Darting a glance to where Otón was just closing the hood of a vehicle beyond the intended victim, Manuel was grateful that they had no family resemblance to indicate they were brothers. Stylishly dressed, by some quirk of hereditary, he was tall, slim and looked like the Anglo ancestor who was responsible for his physical appearance. His sibling, clearly Hispanic in origin, possessed a medium sized and stocky build and had on oil-stained dark blue coveralls inscribed, 'DIEGO'S REPAIR SERVICE' which further reduced the chance of their connection being suspected. His second brother was Otón's close to identical twin, but their filial likeness was rendered less discernible by Rafael being a short distance away. Being the best driver, he was already seated in the first car they had selected to be stolen and was ready to offer a means of escape if they had to take flight without their vehicles for any reason.

Seeing the quick gesture made by Manuel after having opened the door of the sedan, Otón knew he had elected to add to their loot by mugging the well dressed woman. The decision did not come as any surprise. Nevertheless, remembering what had happened during the attempted mugging which had caused them to leave San Antonio and decide the visit to Mexico was necessary, he looked cautiously around. A glance satisfied him that Rafael had also deduced what was contemplated by their older brother and, although it had not been necessary in the forays they had carried out at the parking lots of shopping malls in the East Shore and Evans Hill Districts of Gusher City, he was ready to make the kind of hurried departure used effectively to save them from capture when things had gone wrong in other parts of Texas.

Watching Manuel following the woman, the youngest of the brothers hoped the mugging would be accomplished without the need for assistance from their sibling. Particularly when high on a fix of cocaine – to which all three had graduated from the smoking of *marijuana*, claimed by numerous celebrities of 'liberal' persuasions to be harmless, non-addictive and even beneficial – Otón tended to react too violently if required to give support and had already knifed three women who offered resistance elsewhere in Texas. The latest incident, at San Antonio six days earlier, had resulted in the death of the victim and a very narrow escape for them. What was more, being seen and the alarm having been raised caused Manuel to leave behind the bag which she was struggling to retain when taking Otón's knife in the kidneys. Abandoning the other two vehicles prepared for driving away and using the third to elude pursuit by the police, after a chase which Rafael had no desire to repeat, they had come to the seat of Rockabye County with the intention of collecting sufficient money to get them across the border and lie low in Mexico for a time.

Satisfied that his brothers knew what he was intending,

having allowed the woman to pass without seeing anything to suggest she suspected his intentions, Manuel strode swiftly and quietly after her. Coming into range, confident his presence was undetected, he grabbed for the bag with his right hand and seized her right forearm just below the elbow with his left to help ensure she released it. Even as he started to tug at the handle and tighten the grip with his other fingers, he discovered that he had made an error of judgement in his summation of the situation. In fact, before he could appreciate that the arm he was grasping had much firmer muscles than he would have expected from the kind of pampered member of wealthy society he assumed her to be, it was too late for the discovery to serve as a warning. His touch provoked an instant and very effective response from the seemingly unsuspecting would-be victim.

The moment that the woman felt her bag being seized, although she immediately released it, the rest of her reaction suggested she was far from being paralysed into immobility by surprise. What was more, it soon became apparent that she considered she possessed sufficient knowledge of self defence to be able to counter the attempt to steal it. Flashing across, her left hand caught Manuel by the right wrist. Proving to have a surprising strength for one who had given a very convincing impression of soft living until that moment, she hauled the captured limb in front of her body towards her left hip. While doing so, having lost the somewhat mincing gait which he had assumed was employed to give her a seductive and youthful air, she just as swiftly passed her right hand beneath his armpit until she was able to grasp his bicep with it and moved her right leg until it was against his.

Allowing the would-be mugger no time to resist her movements, giving a jerk of her head which caused the sunglasses to fly from her face, the woman spun rapidly to her left and began to bend at the waist. Then, with a combination of pulling the trapped arm down and across, while thrusting to the rear with her hips and jerking her right leg against his, she caused him to pass over her back.

On feeling him going beyond his point of balance, she snatched free her hands. However, as he was sent sprawling supine upon the hard surface of the parking lot, being released did not allow him to do more than try to break the full impact of the fall he realized was coming. He was only partially successful. Nevertheless, even though the force with which he landed on the hard concrete drove most of the air from his lungs, he was sufficiently in retention of his faculties to decide his brother would come to his rescue.

Seeing what happened, Otón wasted no time before setting about justifying his sibling's summation. Dipping into the side pocket of the coveralls he was wearing as a disguise, his right hand produced the switch-blade knife which he could wield with deadly effect. As its razor sharp blade sprang open, believing his connection with Manuel was not suspected by the woman, he lunged towards the centre of the alley between the cars where the exertion she had put into the 'shoulder body-drop' throw had caused her to stagger. It was his intention to silence her with the kind of thrust from behind which had prevented his previous victims crying out.

Glancing around as she was coming to a stop, the woman responded to the dangerous threat posed by the second brother with a speed equal to that employed against Manuel. However, for a moment, it seemed she was not behaving with the same competence. Raising her right hand as she was turning to face Otón, instead of adopting a posture which might have allowed her to fend off the attack with the knife, she did nothing more positive than reach up and give a tug at her hair. Ineffectual as this appeared to be, the result proved startling. The entire mass of blonde curls came away in her grasp, exposing the genuine red hair they had concealed until that moment. On being removed, they were flung at the approaching man.

Struck in the face by what was obviously a well made wig, not only was Otón's vision obscured, but he was also too surprised to prevent himself from continuing his rapid advance. Instinct caused him to make a slash with the knife, but it failed to find its hoped for target. Twisting clear of the approaching blade, his would-be victim continued to respond in a way which destroyed the earlier brief impression of having been too frightened to protect herself effectively. In fact, it was obvious that she had acquired a very sound working knowledge of *karate*.

Although the woman did not clench her right hand into a fist, the blow she directed at Otón was something vastly more efficacious than a slap to the face. Keeping her fingers extended and together, but with the thumb curved over the palm, she chopped the edge into his throat as he was blundering by. Then, pivoting with a similarly deft rapidity, she stamped the sole of her left boot against the back of his right knee. Croaking in agony, he lost his hold on the weapon. With his equilibrium destroyed, he was unable to avoid stumbling in the opposite direction to where his brother had fallen and dropping on to his hands and knees. Before he could regain any control over his actions, he received an even harder kick to his raised rump and was propelled face forward to the ground with his head almost touching one of the parked vehicles.

Having rendered her second attacker temporarily innocuous, the woman did not behave as might have been expected. Instead of running to the shopping mall in search of assistance, or even shouting to attract attention, she darted swiftly to where her handbag was lying. However, quickly as she moved, she noticed there could be another threat to her intentions and well being.

Turning over and sitting up, shaking his head in an attempt to clear it, Manuel glared at the approaching 'blonde' who had become a red head. Rage suffused his features and he tried to force himself on to his feet. Guessing what he was meaning to do as she was bending to retrieve the handbag, she straightened and lashed out with her right foot. Flopping back on to his rump, he tried instinctively to grab her rising leg. He moved too slowly in his still somewhat befuddled condition. Caught under the chin by the toe of her right boot, which passed between his reaching hands before they could intervene, the power given to the kick pitched him on to his back once more. However, as she made her second attempt to collect the handbag, she was thwarted by what she realized could prove a more serious danger. Hearing a familiar scream of protesting rubber, she looked in the direction from which the sound originated. Seeing a car pull from its space and gather speed as it was turned towards her, she concluded this was not by chance and its purpose was far from innocent.

Being aware of how effectively his brothers could carry out their respective parts in the intended mugging, Rafael could hardly believe his eyes when he saw both fail to achieve their intentions. Given more time, he might have concluded their downfall had resulted because they had been lulled into a sense of false security by the appearance of the proposed victim and had been taken completely by surprise. In the urgency of the situation, he gave no thought to considering what had gone wrong. Spluttering a profanity, he set the car moving to effect a rescue. As he did so, he saw enough to make him suspect the need was even more imperative than if only the woman was involved. The back doors were thrown open and armed men appeared from inside three micro-buses which had previously appeared to be unoccupied. Although none wore uniforms, Rafael did not doubt they were members of a local law enforcement agency. What was more, if the way she had behaved was any guide, the woman had a similar official status and was acting as a most effective decoy.

Motivated more by realizing that to go in the direction of the fight would take him away from the vehicles disgorging the male officers than by any intention of carrying out his usual part when an escape was required, Rafael drove the car towards where neither of his brothers had yet managed to rise. This also took him in the direction of the woman. However, he concluded from her attempt to retrieve the handbag that it held a weapon and he was satisfied he could prevent her from being able to draw it.

CHAPTER TWO

The youngest of the Santoval brothers was correct in his assumption with regards to the official status of the supposedly harmless victim chosen by Manuel. However, the 'blonde' turned red head was more than just a decoy selected for her gender.

Not only was Woman Deputy Alice Fayde a member of the Rockabye County Sheriff's Office,[1] but she had organized and was in command of the operation intended to bring about their arrest!

In one respect, the trio had only themselves to blame for what was happening!

Because the brothers had never become attached to any organization specializing in the theft of automobiles, they considered it advisable to frequently change the location of their depredations. However, like every habitual criminal, they had been able to discover from others of their kind where to obtain information of use to them in whichever area they intended to visit. Putting their knowledge to use on arrival at Gusher City, they had sought out contacts to learn where they could dispose of the cars and other items they intended to steal prior to going into Mexico.

Unfortunately for the trio, as often happened to criminals, news of their activities was not kept as confidential as they would have liked. Although their meeting with him had been too late to prevent their raids in the East Shore and Evans Hill Districts, a regular informer had told Alice of their relationship, activities and intentions. Knowing he was always reliable, she had contacted the Identification and Criminal Records Division of the Texas Department of Public Safety at Austin, which served as a repository for reports pertaining to illegal activities throughout the Lone Star State. The reply was that their *modus*

1. Information regarding the background and special qualifications of Woman Deputy Alice Fayde is given in: APPENDIX ONE.

operandi suggested they could have been responsible for several similar thefts of three vehicles at a time, in conjunction with the occasional mugging of a woman while these were taking place, which had occurred on the parking lots of shopping malls in various cities.

Although no names or accurate descriptions were in the report from I.C.R., on Alice telling them of it, Sheriff Jack Tragg and Chief of Police Phineas Hogan had agreed with her summation that the number and m.o. of the perpetrators matched those of three men wanted by the authorities in San Antonio for murder and offenses against Article 1421 of the Texas Penal Code.[2] For jurisdictional reasons,[3] as a homicide might be involved in addition to the less serious crime of what some law enforcement agencies called 'Grand Theft, Auto', it was decided that the Rockabye County Sheriff's Office would handle the matter and whatever additional assistance they required was to be supplied by the Gusher City Police Department. In accordance with established policy, as the information had been passed to the red head, she and her partner, Deputy Sheriff Bradford 'Brad' Counter were put in charge of the case.

Alice frequently served in the capacity of detective, due to the Sheriff's Office dealing with all cases of homicide and related crimes in Gusher City as well as throughout the rest of Rockabye County, but the assignment she had been given had not required her to exercise her deductive abilities. The closest she had come to this was to assume she was dealing with three brothers who had never been arrested for the theft of automobiles and, in all probability, worked as free-lances instead of belonging to any organized ring of car thieves. Having nothing more concrete to go on, the way in which she had elected to handle the assignment was the result of her training and practical experience in established law enforcement procedures.

Basing her strategy upon a study of the information supplied by the I.C.R. at Austin – regarding the way in which similar thefts had been carried out elsewhere around the State – and the G.C.P.D.'s reports of the incidents at the two local parking lots, the red head had arranged to have stake-outs at the other parking lots in the city. She was aware that, as a general rule, car thieves concentrated solely upon removing the vehicles and did not take the added risk of carrying out a mugging which might not yield any worthwhile loot. Therefore, she had included in her planning a ploy intended to discover whether the brothers were the perpetrators wanted by the San Antonio Police Department for the murder of a female victim by having decoys available to ascertain whether an opportunity to commit such a robbery would be seized upon.

Remembering her informer had claimed the trio planned to leave the country after having raised extra money, Alice had deduced they would strike at the shopping malls in the more prosperous Divisions of the city in the hope of also finding suitable victims to be mugged. Therefore, she had made the selection for her own participation accordingly. With the help of a specialist at make-up serving with the G.C.P.D.[4] and suitable clothing – including the sunglasses and wig – presented by the most expensive dress shop in Upton Heights, she had given herself an appearance of being wealthy which she had guessed would prove to be an irresistible bait. Waiting at a dis-

2. *Article 1421, Texas Penal Code, 'Theft Of Property Of The Value Of $50.00 Or Over', a felony incurring a penalty of imprisonment from two to ten years.*

3. *An explanation of various types of U.S. law enforcement organizations' jurisdictional authority is given in:* Footnote 2, APPENDIX THREE.

4. *The Officer in question was Sergeant Corey Haynes of the Gusher City Police Department's Records & Information Bureau. Three other occasions when he put his specialized training to use for the Rockabye County Sheriff's Office are recorded in:* THE SIXTEEN DOLLAR SHOOTER, POINT OF CONTACT *and* Part Eleven, 'Preventive Law Enforcement', J.T.'S HUNDREDTH.

tance in the Cadillac coupe loaned by a wealthy friend of her partner, which she had concluded correctly would give added support to her disguise, she had driven on to the parking lot when informed over the radio link-up with the stake-out vehicles that the preparations for stealing cars was being commenced by three young men matching the vague descriptions she had received from I.C.R. and San Antonio.

As Alice had hoped, the tallest of the trio had attempted the mugging. Her disguise and histrionic ability had been sufficient to convince him that he would be robbing a wealthy woman somewhat older and less capable of putting up strenuous resistance than herself and who should prove an easy victim. Having employed the thorough training at unarmed combat acquired since becoming a peace officer, aided by his having been taken in by her appearance, she was able to deal with him. What was more, basing her assumption upon the reports of similar incidents she had read, she had anticipated the knife attack would be forthcoming and was ready to adopt equally effective means to avoid it. However, in one respect, she had been lucky. Despite what he had seen, probably because his senses were dulled by the narcotics he had taken before coming to the parking lot, Otón had failed to draw any conclusions from what had happened to his brother and did not expect to meet with the competent resistance he had encountered. Therefore, she had been able to counter both attempts to assault her more easily than would otherwise have been the case.

Despite her success so far, even though the red head knew help would soon be forthcoming from the male peace officers whom she had instructed to conceal themselves in suitable vehicles around the parking lot, she had had no intention of continuing to rely upon her bare hands as a means of protecting herself against her attackers until they could intervene. Unfortunately, the need to cope with Manuel a second time had prevented her from obtaining a most effective means of self preservation by retrieving the handbag and extracting the Colt Commander .45 automatic pistol which reposed inside it. Nor, a glance along the alley between the vehicles informed her, would she be permitted to do so now she had renderd him *hors de combat*.

The car which had attracted Alice's attention when it was set into motion was coming along the gap between the parked vehicles towards her at an increasing speed. Looking through the windshield, she ascertained that it was driven by a man with Hispanic features much like those of her second would-be assailant. Amongst the other details, her informer had remarked upon two of the brothers being almost identical twins. Noticing the resemblance, she surmised that he might be coming in the hope of effecting a rescue. In which case, as he was certain to be sufficiently 'street-wise' to have guessed she was a peace officer, he would realize this could only be achieved if she was prevented from intervening. On the other hand, even if he had only selected his direction because of a desire to avoid the well armed male officers from the micro-buses, he would be equally disinclined to let her delay his departure.

For the red head to draw her conclusions and act upon them took only a couple of seconds. Realizing she would not have sufficient time to arm herself with the Colt Commander, she made no attempt to do so. Hoping the informer was correct in the claim that the taller of her assailants was a brother of the Hispanic twins in spite of his Anglo appearance, which she had deduced would reduce the chances of their connection being suspected by the intended victims of their muggings, she based her tactics upon the relationship. Relying upon the filial attachment to save her, she stepped swiftly to where her first assailant was lying supine and motionless. Standing astride his body and facing the oncoming car, she placed her outside foot on his chest in a way which meant it could only strike her by running over him.

Despite his summations regarding her official status,

once again Rafael found himself startled by the very effective response from the woman he too had first believed to be a harmless victim. Feeling sure the handbag held a firearm of some kind, as it was highly unlikely a female officer acting as a decoy would be without weapons, he had intended to run her down if she had attempted to go and pick it up or do anything else to impede his flight. Seeing the position she had adopted, he decided she was not intending to try and stop him. However, even if he had been so inclined, the way she was standing rendered it impossible for him to run her down without at least seriously injuring his older brother. Nor, a glance in the appropriate direction informed him, would he even be able to rescue his twin. Although Otón was conscious, unlike Manuel, he was still clearly too dazed to move with the kind of speed required for a pick up under the prevailing conditions.

Accepting that rescuing either sibling would be impossible, Rafael did no more than yell a profanity at the red head as he was driving by. Watching through the rear view mirror, he saw her dart forward and scoop up the handbag. As she was reaching inside it, some instinct caused him to look to the front. The sight which met his gaze drove all thoughts of the possible danger she was posing from his head.

CHAPTER THREE

Under different circumstances, Rafael Santoval would not have been unduly perturbed by the masculine figure which lunged from between two vehicles some thirty yards ahead!

Having golden blond hair cut fairly short, and tanned, almost classically handsome features, the young man would be a good six foot three inches in height and had the tremendously wide shouldered, slim waisted build of a contestant in a 'Mr Universe' competition. Like the clothing worn by the red head, his casual attire was clearly made from the best materials Upton Heights had to offer. To obtain such an excellent fit, his lightweight dark blue and green tartan sports jacket must have been cut to his build by a top class tailor. The same applied to the glossy open necked navy blue shirt embellished by a scarlet cravat which could only be silk and his dark grey flannels. The latter were supported by a wide brown waist belt with the floral decorative pattern which was the speciality of master leatherworker, John Bianchi of Temecula, California, and sported a large oval silver buckle inscribed 'BC'. Their legs hung outside Western style boots made from centre-cut ostrich hide and were the kind commanding a high price at every source from which they could be obtained.

Except for two things, the blond giant had the appearance of a well paid young executive from one of the city's more lucrative businesses whose hobby was 'pumping iron' to attain an exceptional physical development. The first indication to the contrary was the silver and gold five pointed star insignia of a deputy sheriff hanging from the breast pocket of the tartan jacket. In the heat of the moment, Rafael might have overlooked it and its indication that the blond did not come into such an innocuous category as first impressions suggested and who, for all his great size, might be driven or knocked aside without difficulty by aiming the vehicle straight at him. However, no amount of stress could have prevented the youngest Santoval brother seeing the short barrelled Winchester Model of

1897 pump action riot gun in his hands. What was more, the speed with which he snapped the butt to his shoulder warned he was almost certain to be proficient in its use.

While each was wearing equally expensive attire, there was one major difference between the way in which Deputy Sheriff Bradford 'Brad' Counter and Woman Deputy Alice Fayde were clothed at that moment. Being possessed of private means in addition to his salary as a peace officer, everything he had on was his own property. Nevertheless, far from being a mere dilettante who had obtained his appointment through family influence and treated it as nothing more than an exciting pastime, he had proven himself to be fully competent at his duties. What was more, Rafael had been correct in the second assumption. He was rated as one of the most skilled handlers of firearms in the law enforcement agencies of Rockabye County.[1]

Brad had been seated in a car at the side of the parking lot nearest to the shopping mall. Although he was unable to see what was taking place, he too had remained in wireless communication with the officers in the micro-buses. Learning that the 'caper was going down' and that Alice's deception was starting to show signs of proving effective, he had left his position. Employing the skill he had acquired in hunting a variety of alert wild animals, and helped by the brothers being occupied with the red head, he had succeeded in avoiding detection as he was making for the alley between the vehicles.

Following the established procedure of almost every law enforcement agency in the United States, knowing they were dealing with men who had already killed and might have the means of fighting back, the blond giant and the other male officers had come prepared to handle such a contingency. Not one of them was relying upon his

1. Information regarding the family background and qualifications of Deputy Sheriff Bradford 'Brad' Counter can be found in the various volumes of the Rockabye County *series.*

basically defensive handgun. They were aware that the mere display of arms such as riot guns, M1 carbines and Armalite M-16 automatic rifles meant for offensive purposes, often had an unnerving effect upon criminals and brought about a surrender without the need to open fire. Or, if this failed and resistance with firearms was attempted, they were equipped to prevent the situation from deteriorating.

Although the blond giant was ready to supply whatever assistance his partner might need, he had selected his supportive weapon to meet the requirements of his main duty of countering – no pun intended – any attempt by the brothers to escape in one of the vehicles selected to be stolen. According to the report of the killing in San Antonio, it was advisable to try and prevent this happening. Commenting upon the skill of the man driving the get-away vehicle, there had been a warning that he had shown a complete disregard for the lives of everybody regardless of age and sex encountered along the route he had taken. In fact, the complete recklessness he had shown in that respect had been a major factor in the trio being able to avoid capture.

Despite the Sheriff's Office having newer and more sophisticated weapons designed for the same purpose, offering either semi or fully automatic instead of manual operation, Brad preferred to rely upon the Winchester Model of 1897 riot gun. Many of his associates considered it close to obsolete, but he claimed its type of mechanism offered a greater control over its rate of fire. Advancing until he was standing directly in the path of the oncoming vehicle on feet spread almost to the width of his shoulders he was aware that his own and the lives of other people might depend upon his being able to justify his selection.

Looking along the twenty inch barrel, which was equipped with a set of sights not usually found on a shotgun intended for purely sporting purposes, the blond giant tightened his right forefinger on the trigger. However, even though the car was coming straight at him and he felt sure it would not be turned aside if he remained where he was standing, his point of aim was not the driver. The Winchester crashed, expelling a solid slug which flew, as intended, to burst through the radiator of the approaching vehicle and shattered the fan. However, the hit did not bring the car to a stop immediately. Nor had he expected to achieve such an effect. In fact, he had loaded two different kind of shells into the weapon with such a contingency in mind!

While Brad was controlling the not inconsiderable recoil kick, his left hand was operating the 'trombone' slide mechanism. By the time that the spent case was removed and a 'live' shell had been transferred from the tubular magazine into the chamber, he had brought down and adjusted the alignment of the barrel. The selection he made was governed by seeing where his partner was positioned in relation to the car. Knowing the second load was not a single slug, he was aware of a possible danger to her. Pointed downwards at a more acute angle than previously, the shotgun barked again. This time nine .32 calibre buckshot balls were sent from its ten gauge muzzle. With the rest ricocheting from the hard concrete surface of the parking lot into the bottom of the vehicle, three of them pierced the inner side of the right front wheel's tyre. Even though it deflated and caused a swerve, the second shot also failed to stop the car.

Swiftly as considerable training had taught the blond giant to operate the Winchester's action, there was no time for him to do so again. However, proving he was neither clumsy nor slow moving in spite of his great bulk, he leapt clear of the still fast moving vehicle. His evasion had not been a moment too soon and he barely missed being struck by the hood in passing. Reloading as he alighted, he pivoted and fired two more shots. Although there was only a brief interval between them, he had changed his aim after the first was discharged and both rear tyres received buckshot balls which reduced the car to running on the rims of the wheels. Nor, despite seeing that the vehicle in which he had hidden had been brought to block the mouth of the gap, did he consider he had inflicted unnecessary damage. During the chase in San Antonio, the driver had rammed and knocked aside a police vehicle which had been in the way and Brad did not doubt a similar attempt would be made if the opportunity was presented.

Such, in fact, had been Rafael's intention when he saw the car drawing to a halt across the opening which would otherwise have offered a chance to reach safety. He realized that the damage inflicted by the first two shots would prevent him from attaining the speed he required and would bring the vehicle to a stop in a short distance, but he did not change his mind. Instead, watching the two men he knew were peace officers dismounting on the side away from him, he elected to ram into the obstacle. If he was lucky, he could disable the pair and make his get-away on foot. However, even as he was applying pressure to the accelerator to build up more speed, he felt and heard the rear tyres burst.

Immediately, the vehicle slowed to a speed at which Rafael knew his purpose could not hope to succeed. What was more, the men from the car blocking his path were lining an Armalite and an M1 carbine across the bonnet and he realized it was himself, not some part of his vehicle they were selecting as their target. Although he too had imbibed narcotics before setting out to raid the shopping mall, he was not made reckless. If they had only been armed with handguns, he might have continued with his attempt. Faced by much more potent weapons and with his car having suffered further damage, he could envisage the intended ramming was doomed to failure and he was likely to be fatally shot if he continued. Accepting the inevitable, he lifted his foot from the accelerator. As the vehicle lurched to a halt, he hurriedly shoved open the door and emerged with hands raised above his head. Glancing over his shoulder, he discovered that neither of his brothers had contrived to escape.

CHAPTER FOUR

On retrieving her handbag, Woman Deputy Alice Fayde quickly slid her Colt Commander from its holster. When selecting the accoutrements for her disguise, she had declined the offer of several bulky rings to accompany the necklace and bracelets. While they might have given the trio an added inducement to attempt the mugging, she had known they would be an impediment to handling the big black automatic and she had elected to wear the gloves instead. Being made of a thin material, these allowed her to grasp the slab-sided butt with the same facility as if she had been bare handed.

As was always the case when the red head was on duty, the weapon was fully loaded, cocked and had the safety catch applied. Pushing down the stud with her right thumb, while tossing aside the bag with her left hand, she assessed the situation quickly. The man at her feet was still unconscious and she was confident that she could leave Deputy Sheriff Bradford 'Brad' Counter's section of the stake-out group to deal with the brother who was attempting to escape in a car. Satisfied on those points, she gave her full attention to the would-be assailant who had wielded the knife. He had already dragged himself to his feet and a raw, almost animalistic, fury was twisting at his less than prepossessing face. Glaring at her, he crouched and, although he had not retrieved the weapon, made a gesture suggesting that any attack he launched might not be with his bare hands.

'Don't *try* it, *hombre*!' the red head warned with the accent of a native born Texan. Raising the Colt to shoulder height, she lined it in a double handed grip which allowed accurate sighting. Alert to the possible danger, she paid no attention to the double crash of the riot gun further along the gap between the vehicles; although when Brad fired twice more a few seconds later she was relieved at realising he had not been struck by the car. Instead, giving all her attention to the man she was confronting, she put an even grimmer timbre to her voice and went on, 'Assume the posture, you're *busted*!'

Listening to the words and watching the action which accompanied them, Otón Santoval regarded both with mixed emotions. Like Rafael, unless he was high on cocaine, he possessed a well developed streak of caution. The rough handling he had already received at the hands of their intended victim had reduced the effect of the 'fix' he had taken before coming to the parking lot. Therefore, while one part of him demanded that he sought revenge upon her, a stronger instinct warned him that doing so would be more than foolish. Even if she was as harmless as he and his brothers had envisaged, it was unlikely he could achieve his desires. There was not only her attitude of readiness to support his supposition. Although they were still some distance away, several well armed men wearing badges were converging upon him.

Having discarded the thought of revenge for its own sake, a second suggestion to strike Otón was that he might grab the woman and use her as a hostage whose life could be bargained for him being allowed to get away. He had a second knife in the left side pocket of his coveralls and, despite her having displayed an unexpected knowledge of unarmed combat, it might work if she was a soft and pampered Upton Heights' socialite who could be terrified into submission by threats of death or disfiguration. However, even though he believed he would be able to draw the knife and reach her before the men were close enough to intervene, he realized there was a serious objection to such a course. The fact that she had worn a wig, the way she had fought off himself and Manuel during the abortive mugging and was now handling the heavy automatic pistol all indicated she too was a peace officer. In which case, she might suspect he was still armed and, guessing what he was contemplating, be ready to counter the attempt.

'Don't even *think* of coming at me!' Alice continued, seeing a trace of uncertainty on the sullen brown face as the young man's left hand made a movement in the direction of the near side pocket of his coveralls, confirming her suspicion that he was still armed. Lowering the Commander slowly and deliberately into a different point of alignment, she elaborated, 'You'll get hit where it'll *hurt* if you take just one step this way.'

Staring at the big automatic and halting the attempt to reach the knife, Otón did not consider there was any consolation to be drawn from the muzzle – which seemed to be *far* larger than its not inconsiderable .45 calibre – no longer being pointed in a rock steady fashion straight at the centre of his forehead. The weapon was still lined at him, but its target was obviously *much* lower down. With a chilling sensation, he drew a conclusion regarding exactly where the new point of aim might be. Nevertheless, although he had often heard how painful was the effect of a bullet in the stomach before it proved fatal, such a possibility was not the cause of his perturbation.

A rumour was currently circulating the underworld, having been given strength by an incident in a television 'police' series highly regarded in criminal circles for its policy of always selecting plots intended to make law enforcement agencies look at their worst. It was claimed that female peace officers, having grown disenchanted by the courts showing excessive leniency when dealing with men who had carried out vicious sexual attacks upon women, were training with their handguns until becoming capable of hitting the most vulnerable portion of the male anatomy thus preventing any chance of such an offense being repeated.

Otón was one criminal who did not doubt the rumour was founded on truth!

Studying the coldly implacable features of the red head, which the excessive make-up enhanced rather than concealed, the young man did not doubt she had attained such skill. He was equally convinced by her attitude and tone that she was hoping to be given an excuse to put her training to use. Although one part of him still suggested he should draw the knife and rush at her, not even the remnants of the false courage induced by his most recent fix were proof against disturbing thoughts of emasculation should the attempt be made. Nor did he respond to a second mental proposal that he should seek to avoid arrest by running away. He suspected that, as soon as he tried to turn, she would be only too willing to use the movement as an excuse to squeeze the trigger and inflict the most terrible kind of injury he could envisage.

'S – stay cool, lady!' Otón yelled, accepting escape was impossible and thrusting his hands hurriedly above his head. 'You've *got* me!'

'I sure as hell *have*!' Alice confirmed, without lowering her Colt from its deliberately selected alignment. 'Assume the posture!'

After the third of the Santoval brothers had turned to lean with arms extended across the hood of the nearest vehicle and legs wide apart, the red head gave a sigh of satisfaction. For a moment, having had sufficient experience with 'users' of 'hard' narcotics to suspect he came into that category, she had thought he might still be sufficiently 'high' to try and attack her with the knife she suspected he was carrying. Having no wish to shoot if it could be avoided, she had adopted means which she hoped would remove the need. She too was cognizant with the rumour which had brought about the fear she sought in her opponent. That was why she had changed her point of aim and given a very convincing suggestion to make him believe she was ready and even eager to carry it out. Her gamble had produced the desired result.

A glance around informed Alice that everything else was under control. As she had guessed, but was still relieved to discover it was true, her partner had evaded the car and was now going to help the other two members of his group to secure the driver. The officers from the micro-buses were almost on hand to take charge of her would-be attackers. Although she did not doubt that all the captured trio were fully conversant in English, each party had an officer of Hispanic birthright to 'read their rights' to them in Spanish. This was precaution taken to circumvent the ploy frequently used by defense attorneys since the Supreme Court had delivered what was known in law enforcement circles as the 'Miranda Decision'. When a non-Anglo defendant was brought to trial, it would be claimed he was unable to speak sufficient English to understand what he was told when this now essential legal procedure was being carried out after his arrest. Therefore, he was unaware of his 'rights' under the Constitution of the United States and could not be tried for his crime.

All in all, the red head considered she had done a good afternoon's work. The capable way in which she set up the stake-out had led to the arrest of three vicious and dangerous criminals. Although it had been necessary to damage one vehicle to prevent the escape of the third brother, she considered this was preferable to allowing him to get out of the parking lot and endanger lives during a chase through the streets of the city.[1] Furthermore, by putting herself at risk as a decoy, she had established a possible connection between the trio and the murder of the woman in San Antonio.

However, unlike so many plots of classic detective fiction, the successful outcome had not been achieved by deductive reasoning, searching for clues, nor even questioning of suspects until one made an incriminating statement. The assignment had required only a knowledge of where to obtain information regarding the activities of the trio elsewhere in Texas, plus an ability to make arrangements based upon their m.o. which covered most possible contingencies to ensure they would be captured wherever in Gusher City they struck. In fact, such was generally the

1. Being what 'liberals' term a 'redneck' and, therefore, a stout believer in the enforcement of law and order, the owner raised no objections when discovering what had happened to his vehicle. He stated that, not only would making good the damage be covered by his insurance, but he considered it a small price to pay for the removal of three such dangerous criminals.

case in law enforcement work as she knew it.

Watching the final stages of the operation being concluded, Alice did not realize she was to be involved in another even more dangerous operation, but without the opportunity for such careful advance planning, before many days had passed!

Furthermore, it would be one which would call for the exercise of deductive reasoning![2]

2. *Recorded in:* Part Four, 'No Man About The House', MORE J.T.'S LADIES.

PART TWO

AMANDA 'THE SCHOOL SWOT' TWEEDLE
In
A CASE OF BLACKMAIL

CHAPTER ONE

'BENKINSOP'S ACADEMY FOR
THE DAUGHTERS OF GENTLEFOLK'S
DEBATING SOCIETY PRESENTS
AN INTER-SCHOOL DEBATING EVENING
BETWEEN
BENKINSOP'S
and
LOWER GREBE A.S.G.'S O.G.A.
CULMINATING IN
A GRAND TAG TEAM DEBATE
"BENKERS' BLONDE BOMBSHELLS"
PENELOPE PARKERHOUSE
& Ms MARGARET LEICESTER
vs.
"THE SCREWS OF LOWER GREBE A.S.G."
Ms ANN DULVERTON & Ms. STEPHANIE THORPE'

Charles Tremayne – television critic for the *Daily Twinkle* – read the announcement printed in bright red letters on the poster at the entrance when he arrived. Even if he had not been informed already of the fact by his host, the wording certainly suggested something different from the usual conventional evening of debates between two schools. Furthermore, holding the 'debates' in the modern building of the Physical Education Department and not the magnificent large Georgian mansion which housed the main portion of Benkinsop's Academy For The Daughters Of Gentlefolk made it quite plain the evening was to be an unusual one.

In the first place, the gymnasium had had most of its equipment moved back to make room for the chairs occupied by a large number of well dressed and obviously wealthy spectators. Nor was the only item of equipment left in the centre of the large room what one would have expected to find in such an establishment. The audience were seated around a full sized boxing ring and not in front of the kind of raised dais generally used for an evening of debates between the pupils – 'old girls', where Lower Grebe A.S.G. was concerned – of two schools. What was more, they were not listening attentively and restricting themselves to polite applause when some shrewd point or argument was made. Instead, they were giving surprisingly loud and regular vocal encouragement which, it must be confessed, did not appear to be distracting the four latest contenders in the slightest.

The behaviour of the audience was not the only 'different' thing about the evening. While Tremayne's sexual proclivities were not in accord with the majority of the male members of the audience – who found the appearance of some members of the opposing teams in the latest debate just as attractive as their predecessors – it had to be admitted the attire they wore was far from the fashion normally regarded as acceptable for conventional debates. Nor were they conducting their discussion orally, with the exception of occasional yells, squeals of pain or anger, gasps and grunts.

At that moment, swinging Ms. Ann Dulverton around by the hair at arms' length, Penelope Parkerhouse – known as 'Penny' to her schoolmates, although she was 'Head Girl' and captain of Benkinsop's Debating Society – yielded to the objections of the male adjudicator and opened her hands. Waiting until Ann ran backwards against and rebounded from the padded turnbuckle in a corner of the ring, Penny darted to meet her. Bounding into the air with a shriek of delight, the Head Girl continued to express her point of view in the discussion by delivering what, in the kind of 'debating' they were engaged in, was described as a 'dropkick'. Caught in the bosom by the soles of her specialized debating footwear, which crushed the mounds and elicited a squeal of pain, the recipient was pitched into the corner again.

Thirty-five years of age, five foot three in height and good looking, Ann Dulverton had yellowish red hair in a tightly curled bouffant pile. Glistening with sweat and marred by signs of mingled anger and suffering, her features were good looking. She had a curvaceous and sturdy close to buxom build, shown to its best advantage by the one-piece glossy black swimsuit which – along with matching conventional ankle length 'ring boots' – comprised her only costume. Cut with a daring décolleté and low at the back, the thin material fitted as though it was moulded to her rather than merely donned. Firmly fleshed and well muscled, albeit not to the point of losing femininity, she was obviously in the peak of physical condition.

Although three inches shorter than her opponent and younger by eighteen years, having her ash blonde hair in a frizzy bubble cut on top of her head made Penny appear almost the same height. Glistening with freely shed perspiration and showing signs of exertion, her face was pretty and suggestive of a zestful love of life. Dressed in the same fashion, except her swimsuit and ring boots were white, her extremely well defined contours also qualified for the designation 'hour-glass'. Despite the difference in their ages, the size of Penny's bosom exceeded that of Ann's and was firm and out-thrust against the plunging neckline of her costume. Below it, her waist was trim and her hips filled out curvaceously, being set upon sturdily well formed legs. These, like her arms, showed the play of potent muscles and she too clearly exercised sufficiently to keep herself in trim.

While the latest arguments to be employed in the debate were extremely painful, the red head, striking the turnbuckle and being thrust forward again, proved she was not rendered incapable of retaliation. Swerving aside as Penny – always impetuous – once again darted towards her, she did more than just avoid the arms reaching to grab her. Swinging up her bent right leg, she rammed the top of its bulky thigh into the Head Girl's midsection. Giving vent to a croaking gasp, Penny folded at the waist with both hands clutching at the point of impact. Blundering past her assailant, it was her turn to be brought to a halt by colliding with the corner post. However, instead of following up her advantage, Ann swung around and crossed to touch the hand which her partner in the debate was holding over the uppermost of the three horizontal ropes in her direction.

Stephanie 'Stevie' Thorpe, having remained on the apron of the ring at the corner where the turnbuckle was covered in bright red, and holding the three foot length of thin Manila cord attached to the top of the padded post in compliance with the rules for the tag team debate, now vaulted over the ropes as soon as the requisite contact was made with Ann. Five foot four and thirty-two years of age, she too was good looking; albeit just a trifle sharp featured and with an expression suggesting a stern, commanding nature. In the course of the 'debate', the bun into which her blonde hair had been tightly drawn back was now almost destroyed by the treatment to which it had been subjected. Filling her black swimsuit just as adequately and attractively as the other three, she had a well rounded close to buxom physique and, by a slight margin, its muscular development was the best of the contending quartet of debaters.

Dashing across the ring to where Penny was turning, Stevie caught her by the wrists and pushed her against the turnbuckle. Pulled forward while her assailant was deliberately sinking rump first on to the padded white canvas floor of the ring, the Head Girl had two feet placed against her stomach and received a thrust which catapulted her through the air. Turning an involuntary half somersault, she descended on her back and bounced to the ropes at the opposite side. Nor was that the end of her troubles. Bouncing up with a rubbery agility, Stevie hurried across and buried both hands into Penny's ash blonde locks. Jerked erect in a painful fashion, before the adjudicator could protest over the infringement of the rules for the debate, she received a forearm smash to the jaw which dumped her on the canvas again. Putting a hand on the face of the small man who was officiating and pushing him away, Stevie repeated the line of argument she had just employed with an equally painful result.

Leaning over the ropes at the corner which had a royal blue turnbuckle, but ensuring she did not release the length of thin Manila cord in accordance with the rules, Ms Margaret Leicester yelled indignant protests over such unfair debating. She was an inch taller than her partner and thirty-five years old. However, having her platinum blonde hair in a close and boyish urchin crop made her seem shorter and almost dwarfed by her opponents. Despite the opportunities for over-indulgence offered by her position as the school cook, the well rounded contours of her 'hour-glass' figure – displayed just as advantageously by an equally daring white costume – were firmly fleshed and she was just as clearly in excellent physical condition.

Once again the adjudicator moved forward, catching Stevie by the arm in an attempt to prevent her continuing with the illicit line of reasoning. Shaking herself free, she hauled Penny up for the third time. However, the brief respite had given the Head Girl an opportunity to decide upon a counter-argument. Allowing herself to be brought to her feet, she folded and swung her right fist so that the knuckles were buried in her would-be assailant's *solar plexus*, despite such a way of making a point being no more legal than the treatment which had befallen her.

Letting out a gasp, Stevie doubled over and turned away. She had the sole of Penny's left ring-boot placed against the tightly stretched black material covering her rump and received a push which sent her in a headlong sprawl which ended with her almost going through the ropes. Gingerly fingering her chin, which throbbed from the impact of the two forearm smashes it had suffered, the Head Girl ran over to touch hands and allow her co-debater to replace her. Doing so, Margaret proved she too did not believe in strict compliance with all the rules by crossing and trying to shove Stevie all the way out of the ring with her foot.

'Good for you, Maggie, boot her right out!' yelled Maxwell "Big Max" Spender, sitting in the place of honour at the right side of the Headmistress. Tall, burly and distinguished looking, his dark hair was turning grey at the temples. Clad in an excellently cut black dinner jacket, there was nothing to show he was known to Scotland Yard as the current "managing director" of the South London and Southern England Crime Consortium. Lowering his voice, although he was expressing a similar sentiment to many of the spectators, he went on, 'They're doing well, considering who they're up against, Amelia.'

'I expected they would,' replied Miss Amelia Penelope Diana Benkinsop, G.C., M.A., B.Sc. (Oxon), who – as was implied by the name given to the team in the latest debate – was known to her respectful and admiring pupils as "Benkers", although not to her face. Her slightly husky voice had an upper class accent which had no trace of affectation, and which she had come by naturally. 'Cook and Penelope compliment one another's debating techniques so well. But I do *wish* they wouldn't get so carried away they forget the rules of good sportswomanship.'

While some of the other women in the hall might seek to prove they were better endowed physically, to the extent of employing artificial aids in a few cases, none could match the sheer presence of the Headmistress and owner of the school. Her age was indeterminate beyond indications that she was in the prime of life. Neither too tall nor too short in height, she had golden blonde hair treated with the kind of ultra elegance which a very prominent *coiffeur* in London's West End created, feeling privileged to be summoned from his place of business and attend to her at the school. It set off her flawless beauty and emphasised the regal distinction of her patrician features perfectly. Regardless of its décoleté being decorous, especially in comparison with some of the other members of her sex who were present, her sleeveless and contour-hugging royal blue cocktail dress neither sought to distract from, nor draw attention to, her extremely curvaceous – and natural – figure. What was more, although less in quantity than some of the distaff side of the audience, her jewellery was the most expensive in the gymnasium and in the best of taste.

'Why don't you have Amanda team up with Penny?' Spender inquired, wondering where the girl to whom he was referring might be.

'Good heavens, I couldn't do *that*, no other debating team would have a *chance*,' Miss Benkinsop replied and, suspecting the interest in the absence of her star pupil, the "school swot", Amanda Tweedle, sought to avoid being questioned about it. 'By the by, Maxwell, who is that *dreadful* little man Mr Pearman brought with him?'

'Name's Charles Tremayne,' Spender supplied, looking over his shoulder to where the men in question were seated a couple of rows to his rear. 'He's the television critic for the *Daily Twinkle*.'

'I *never* read it and, even if I did by some mischance, I wouldn't read the *television critic's* column,' Miss Benkinsop asserted. 'Going by the drivel they turn out, particularly where any programme popular with the public is concerned, they *all* suffer from delusions of adequacy and it's my opinion they are only given that task because they aren't competent to do anything which requires brains, intelligence, or ability. I wonder why Mr Pearman brought him?'

'John-Boy's daughter wants to be an actress,' Spender answered. 'Didn't he send her here?'

'Only for a term,' the headmistress admitted. 'I suggested she might be *happier* somewhere which would cater better for her "permissive" attitudes and he removed her. However, I can't remember her showing any particular interest in, or talent for, acting. Or *anything* else, for that matter.'

'That doesn't surprise me,' Spender sniffed disdainfully. 'Like father, like daughter, I've always heard. Anyway, she's set on becoming an actress and he probably thinks Tremayne, knowing the TV crowd, can help her get some parts.'

'They do seem to be overly impressed by television critics,' Miss Benkinsop said dryly. 'Would you drop a hint to Mr Pearman that I would much *prefer* he doesn't make a habit of bringing such people here please, Maxwell? He's not *our* type of person at all.'

Even as Spender was nodding concurrence, his attention was drawn back to the tag team debate. Having been brought to order by the adjudicator, Margaret had withdrawn to the centre of the ring. Saved from falling out and pushed back by Ann, Stevie was getting to her feet. Watching the two blondes come to grips, Miss Benkinsop decided she had done all that was necessary with regards to John Pearman's uninvited guest and put the matter from her thoughts.

The Headmistress would not have been either so complacent or relaxed if she had known the real reason Tremayne had prevailed upon his compaion to bring him to the Debating Evening!

CHAPTER TWO

For almost fifteen minutes after the conversation between Miss Amelia Benkinsop and Maxwell Spender, the tag team debate was continued with unabated, vigorously expressed, points of view and counter arguments in rapid succession. What is more, despite being at a slight disadvantage in height and weight, 'Benkers' Blonde Bombshells' had already established that they were not out-classed no matter whether engaged at debating in strict accordance with the rules or with the kind of tactics which had aroused the Headmistress's disapproval. Proving they were very well trained, they employed their somewhat greater skill and marginally superior co-operation to offset the extra size and strength of their opponents. However, because of possessing mutually competitive spirits and being imbued by the same desire to score a victory – either by what *aficionados* of the Benkinsop variety of debating termed a pinfall, a submission, or a knockout – there had been occasional infringements of the code of conduct which compelled the male adjudicator to punish both teams with a public rebuke.

Being so evenly matched, the only periods throughout the debate when at least two of the shapely contenders were not involved in a continuous very lively and active discussion was when one of them found herself trapped by action being carried out in such a painful fashion that it forced an admission of defeat, or when one or other of them was held in a manner which resulted in her shoulders being pressed against the canvas floor of the ring while the adjudicator counted to three. Should either contingency successfully occur, the team on the receiving end would be considered to have lost the first session of the debate.

The former contingency almost occurred when, sitting on the floor, Ms Margaret Leicester was trapped from behind with Ms Ann Dulverton's bulkily shapely legs encircling her trim midsection in what was termed a 'scissors'. Nor did the red head rely solely upon the constriction she was applying the achieve the purpose she was seeking. Raised into the air, the platinum blonde was brought down so her thinly protected rump hit the canvas with a resounding thud. After being the victim of three more of this point of view, she contrived to force apart the crossed feet and, by wriggling across the ring without rising, made the contact which permitted Penelope Parkerhouse to replace her.

A short time later, after Ms Stephanie Thorpe had replaced the red head, the Head Girl attained the type of argument which *aficionados* of such debates call a 'Boston crab'. Lying on her stomach, with Penny standing astride her torso, her legs were curled upwards under the girl's arms from behind. The curvature being applied to her spine was sufficiently painful almost to cause her to admit she was defeated by the point being made. However, gritting her teeth and resisting the impulse, employing to its best advantage her extra weight and strength – small though the latter might be – she straightened her limbs in a way which flipped the head girl over and she was free to seek a respite by tagging Ann.

In between these two different types of contention, Ann was at one point knocked over backwards by a charge and leap from Margaret. Coming down, she was close to suffering a pin-fall when the platinum blonde descended across her torso and pressed her shoulders on the canvas. Being marginally the stronger, she contrived to lift first the left and then the right side clear just long enough to stop the count to three which the adjudicator – lying on his stomach and looking underneath her to make sure she was in the correct position – was making and which would have established her defeat. Then, gathering her strength for a more decisive counter-argument, she surged unexpectedly upwards and tossed her somewhat lighter opponent on to him.

Not long after, it was Penny in danger of a similar fate. She was trapped supine, with Stevie lying over her head and upper torso to hold her arms outstretched. Before the adjudicator could complete the requisite count of three, putting to use all the power her curvaceously close to buxom physique could produce, she set about avoiding being pinned by bracing her feet on the canvas. Then, arching her body upwards in spite of the weight pressing on it – which was alleviated slightly by the larger blonde's torso jerking upwards a little for some reason – she rolled them both sideways and they separated.

On getting to her feet, suggesting the reason for the otherwise inexplicable movement which helped defeat her purpose, the blonde representative of 'The Screws Of Lower Grebe A.S.G.' rubbed at the left mound of her imposing bosom. She was protesting to the adjudicator that it had been bitten when Penny resumed the offensive. Any sympathy Stevie might have gained was immediately nullified by her delivering a punch with a clenched fist into the white covered midsection. Nor did the Head Girl receive any expression of condolence from the adjudicator due to her instantaneous and instinctive retaliation in kind being equally an infringement of the rules.

Nor were these the only infractions which had taken place. In fact, both teams were equally guilty of illicit debating methods as individuals and working in conjunction with each other. During the various 'one-on-one' discussions, no matter which combination of contenders were involved, there was some hair pulling, blows with the clenched fist or flat palm and attempts to make a fresh point when the opponent had been thrown to the canvas and released. There had been co-ordinated efforts when, in open defiance of the rules, one of the team came to the assistance of her co-debater without receiving the required touch of hands before doing so.

Once, when Penny was pushed near enough by Ann, Stevie had reached over the ropes to grab her by the hair and hold her so a knee to the stomach could be delivered. Later, making the most of Stevie coming within reaching distance while holding Margaret's head in chancery and bringing up forearm smashes to the bowed forward torso, the Head Girl caught hold of the low cut back of the glossy black swimsuit. The unexpected jerk she gave caused a distraction, allowing her co-debater to get free and repay the legitimate blows with illicit punches. Releasing her hold before the adjudicator was able to discover her misdemeanour, Penny assumed a convincing aura of innocence when he accused her of the infringement.

'What *me*?' the Head Girl objected in a somewhat strident tone, which indicated she was born and raised well within the traditional sound of Bow Bells in London. Mindful that Miss Benkinsop would take umbrage at the use of any stronger language and, regardless of her status in the school, inflict a suitable punishment, she restricted the rest of her comment to, 'I blooming well didn't do *nothing*!'

Instead of continuing with the matter, seeing what was happening behind him, the adjudicator compelled Margaret and Ann to stop what had developed into a fist fight and ordered them to continue debating in a more legal fashion.

With one exception, even if accompanied by his wife or lady friend, every man in the room considered the performances in the tag team debate were skilful and even erotically stimulating. However, Charles Tremayne's prefences along those lines being directed to members of his own sex or children of a more tender age than Penny, made him completely indifferent to the latter consideration. Furthermore, having his kind's snobbish antipathy for *every* form of popular entertainment, he was not interested in the former aspect of the evening's event. At least, not so far as an enjoyable and exciting form of entertainment was concerned.

In his late twenties, tallish and gaunt, the television critic of the *Daily Twinkle* had long and straggly mousey brown hair already going thin on top. Set in a surly frown, his ashy grey face had sunken eyes, hollow cheeks and thick lips which created an effect even his mother might have been excused for not loving. Because of the strict code of dress demanded by Miss Benkinsop, while he had obviously refrained from anything so reactionary as having a wash and shaving off the two-day stubble mandatory for his kind, he had been compelled to don something other than his usual informal and invariably grubby attire. However, he did little justice to the black dinner jacket, matching lace-trimmed trousers, white shirt with a red bow-tie and cummerbund which he had rented. Rather he looked like an indifferent actor playing a butler for a third rate amateur theatre group or in a British television play.

Despite his unprepossessing appearance, suspended beneath the front of the already food stained white shirt and with the lens disguised as one of his oversized black studs, Treymayne had concealed a most sophisticated Russian-made camera of a type designed for use by their spies and loaned to his newspaper for services rendered in a variety of ways. Small and compact, it nevertheless had self focussing lens and a built-in metering system for automatically setting the aperture and shutter speed. Charged with 800 A.S.A. high speed film, it was capable of obtaining excellent photographs in less adequately illuminated locations than the gymnasium, so that, aided by the arc lights overhead, the ring was particularly photogenic.

However, the television critic did not intend to make use of the special features of the spy-camera to obtain pictures of the debates – or even members of the audience – in order to carry out an assignment he had received in his capacity as a member of the *Daily Twinkle's* staff. The editor of the *Daily Twinkle*, although being on *very* close terms with Tremayne regardless of him being a university graduate (albeit one who spent much more time in left wing political agitation than study), considered with justification that Tremayne was incapable of doing any useful kind of reporting or feature writing and so contrived to keep him on the payroll in the only capacity he was capable of filling.

Tremayne had something much more sinister in mind!

Learning of the way in which the 'Debating Evenings' were conducted at Benkinsop's Academy For The Daughters Of Gentlefolk, the television critic persuaded John Pearman – whose sexual proclivities were similar to his own despite being a 'family man' – to invite him to attend. However, his objective was not merely to act as a visitor enjoying a most enjoyable spectacle. He intended to obtain photographs of the debates using the concealed spy-camera, as these might make not only the Headmistress amenable to his scheme, but also such members of the audience who would have no wish for it to become known they had been present at such a function and who would pay handsomely to ensure the fact was not made public.

Although a shrewder person might have wondered how a man like Pearman came to be invited to such an unconventional function at what he had been informed was a very exclusive public school,[1] the thought had never occurred to Tremayne. He knew his host was a criminal. In fact, this was the only reason he had become acquainted with one he considered to be his social and intellectual inferior. Nevertheless, it still came as a surprise – and a disappointment – to discover everybody else in the audience, with the exception of the Headmistress and some of her teaching staff who were in attendance, came into the same category. He had hoped to procure photographs of some prominent people associated with the Conservative Party, particularly if from the Right side of it. Failing that, he would have settled for a potential victim of Liberal or even Social Democratic Party persuasions. However, he had concluded that blackmail would be extremely dangerous to attempt against men he was informed were leading lights in the underworld throughout the British Isles, or

1. For the benefit of American readers, the equivalent of a British 'public school' in the U.S.A. would be a 'private' or 'preparatory' establishment at which the parents also paid a fee to obtain admittance for their offspring.

the visitors of equal stature from the Continent and the United States.

Pondering upon the matter and reaching the conclusion that he should adopt the safer course of trying to sell the photographs and story for use in the Sunday Supplement of the *Daily Twinkle*, the television critic overheard an exchange of confidences on the row of seats in front of him. It suggested he might still be able to use the former for the purposes of blackmail and, failing that, could profit by employing them to illustrate the kind of article his paper took the greatest delight in printing.

'I'll tell you what, Edna,' said a glamorous and shapely red haired woman clad in a daring silver lamé cocktail dress and with expensive looking jewellery liberally bespattering her. She was speaking with a broad Liverpool accent. 'If the screws had been as tough as those two while I was at Lower Grebe, I'd not have fancied myself anywhere nearly so much of a tearaway.'

'I know what you mean,' admitted the blonde occupant of the next chair, who was just as attractive and well adorned, with a voice equally indicative of an upbringing in Birmingham. She too was watching Stevie who had trapped Margaret in a neutral corner and was applying some very rough points of view with her knees and elbows to the body. 'Thorpie and Ginger Dulverton can certainly handle themselves better than any of them who were there while I was inside.'

A feeling of excitement welled through the television critic. Not only was he aware that the other contenders in the debates were members of the Lower Grebe Approved School For Girls' Old Girls Association, but he knew 'screws' was the underworld's name for prison officers of all kinds. While he was sure his paper would be delighted to claim the first category of women were being compelled by an uncaring capitalist monetary society to 'demean' themselves in such a fashion because they were unable to obtain the kind of honest work which the editorial staff pretended to believe they sought, it would be even more delightful to announce two of the wardresses of the establishment were participants.

Based upon past experiences in conducting such negotiations, Tremayne suspected the red head and the blonde co-debaters would be willing to pay as much as they could afford to prevent the information being passed to the appropriate authorities. What was more, judging by all Pearman had said about her, the Headmistress probably possessed what the television critic regarded as being the kind of out-moded upper class notions about responsibilities and *noblesse oblige* which would make her willing to contribute even more money than they would have available to keep 'The Screws Of Lower Grebe A.S.G.' from suffering the consequences of their participation being reported.

While Tremayne was reaching his conclusions, the tag team debate was approaching its climax!

Oblivious of the rules requiring she remained no further from the royal blue corner post than was allowed by retaining a hold on the Manila cord, seeing her co-debater's plight, Penny ducked between the ropes and rushed across to grab Stevie by the arms from behind. However, before the platinum blonde could take advantage of this, Ann discarded the cord in the bright red corner and charged to Stevie's rescue. A moment later, all four were engaged upon a wild tangle of furiously flailing fists and indiscriminately kicking feet more resembling an all-in brawl than a formal debate under Benkinsop's rules.

Trying to intervene, the adjudicator was set upon by both sets of co-debaters and propelled through the ropes. Despite saving himself from dropping to the floor of the gymnasium and coming to his feet, he did not offer to return to the inside of the ring. Instead, having given a shrug of resignation directed to the Headmistress, he turned and leaned with his arms resting on the top strand to watch what was happening from a position of comparative safety.

Much to the delight of the spectators, with the exception of a clearly disapproving Miss Benkinsop and the now slightly more interested television critic, almost three minutes of the fast and furious impromptu debating took place. There were occasions when, so heated had the situation become, the almost unthinking points of view and arguments caused the co-debaters to be in contention against one another instead of their opponents until re-engaging in an equally indiscriminatory fashion. Then, glistening with freely flowing perspiration and their hair resembling wet and dishevelled mops, the contenders broke apart.

In some way, each debater found herself racing back and forwards across the ring under the impulsion of the springiness imparted by the tightly stretched ropes. All were completely out of control and, after a couple of near misses, they converged in the centre of the ring. Four breathless wails of distress rang out as a mutual appreciation of what lay in store was reached. It was ended by their curvaceously close-to-buxom-bodies meeting in a multiple collision which cracked heads against one another and crushed imposing bosoms together with a resounding 'thwack'. Rebounding apart, they all alighted supine with arms and legs thrown apart so they looked like starfish tossed up and discarded on a beach.

Entering the ring, the adjudicator crossed and started to count. It was a mere formality. Not one of the debaters showed any sign of recovering, much less being able to attempt to rise, by the time he reached 'ten', and he announced, to tumultuous applause, the debate was to be considered a draw.

CHAPTER THREE

'Excuse me, ma'am,' said the girl standing in the open door of Miss Benkinsop's study, having knocked and received permission to enter. It was ten o'clock on the morning of the day after the Debating Evening. Her voice had a gentle, somewhat squeaky, timbre perfectly complimenting her demure and respectful attitude. 'May I come in, please?'

'Of course you may, my dear,' the Headmistress confirmed, showing none of the pleasure and pride she always felt when looking at her star pupil. 'Do come in by all means. I was just going to send for you.'

As always in school hours, Miss Benkinsop was wearing a well tailored tweed two-piece costume and an otherwise unadorned frilly bosomed white silk blouse which she nevertheless contrived to make look as attractive and eye-catching as the cocktail gown which had been much admired the previous evening, particularly by all but one male guest. She was seated at a well polished desk which was undoubtedly a valuable antique, yet just as obviously functional. Its top was bare except for an unused sheet of blue blotting paper, an onyx pen-stand and inkwell, a red and a blue telephone and a small box-like apparatus connected to them.

Amanda Tweedle did not possess the requisite family background to to be granted acceptance by Benkinsop's Academy For The Daughters Of Gentlefolk, but she had been there for five years and had just passed her seventeenth birthday. She was in the Sixth Form and had been appointed a Prefect to help enforce discipline. She was the only child of a widower who was a brilliant scientist, albeit one so much in the 'absent-minded professor' mould that he was killed because of a failure to follow the basic precaution of taking cover when testing a new type of high explosive he had concocted.[1] Nevertheless, having delivered her there in the erroneous belief that he had arrived at Roedean, her father went away and met his end before the Headmistress was able to contact him and have the situation rectified. Not even with the assistance of her superlative sources of information had Miss Benkinsop been able to trace a single relation who could assume guardianship and responsibility. Therefore, with her invariable sense of compassion, she had waived her usually most strict conditions of admission and allowed the little orphan to stay.

The decision had proved most beneficial to all concerned!

By virtue of her extraordinary ability to absorb all kinds of knowledge and through an attendance to all her studies far in excess of any of her classmates, Amanda had soon acquired the status of being the 'School Swot'. Not that she was in any way close to the appearance traditionally ascribed in literature – especially 'school' stories in girls papers – to one with such a sobriquet. Convention expected a person imbued by such proclivities to be tall, lanky, plain of features, possibly endowed with numerous pimples, peering owlishly through thick-lensed spectacles and having shoulders rounded as the result of long hours spent poring over books.

Surrounded by a halo of perfectly coiffured blonde hair, Amanda's exceptionally beautiful face bore an expression of demure, almost elfin innocence which could bring

1. Benkinsop's Academy For The Daughters Of Gentlefolk only accepted pupils from the very best criminal families. The offspring of ponces, grasses (informers), drug pushers, white slavers, Socialist millionaires, Labour members of Parliament, Communist trade union officials and television stars famous for expressing left wing views – many of whom in the last four categories sought entry for their daughters despite publicly expressing opposition to such privilege in schooling for the children of others – were never *allowed admittance.*

out the protective masculine instincts of even a most confirmed misogynist. The School's uniform – a navy blue blazer and matching gymslip ending just above knee level, a white blouse, red, white and blue striped necktie, black stockings and well polished shoes having heels of moderate height as required by Miss Benkinsop – could not conceal that inside the garments was a body with superlative feminine contours.

Nevertheless, although five foot seven, the School Swot conveyed the impression of being very small and helpless!

Nothing was further from reality and the appearance was certainly deceptive!

Amanda had attained an almost omniscient erudition, to which she was constantly adding, and was capable of putting everything she learned to practical use. Among numerous other things, in addition to possessing a knowledge many a top-rated mechanic would be hard pressed to duplicate, she could handle a powerful car as well as any leading driver on the international Grand Prix circuits, or – as Maxwell Spender had once put it – the best 'wheel man' employed to ensure a safe getaway after a robbery. What was more, not only did she have a knowledge and practical ability at unarmed combat which put to shame the toughest 'minders' of the underworld, she had also proven herself equally adept in the use of every type of hand-held weapon.

As usual when entering the most sacrosanct portion of the entire school, even on those rare occasions when she was summoned there to answer for some piece of mischief in which she – invariably in the company of Penelope Parkerhouse, her closest friend – had taken part, Amanda experienced a comforting sensation of being at home.

Decorated and furnished to the height of refinement, combining the subtle blend of luxury with utility created by the desk in its centre, the large room somehow retained the atmosphere of all its functions. It was, as the situation warranted, a sitting-room for the entertainment of visitors, a study and the business office from which the affairs of the establishment were conducted. Hopeful and actual parents of pupils were interviewed there. The girls knew it to be the place where praise or punishment for misdeeds was meted out, the latter always well deserved and never more excessive than the situation demanded, but also forgotten when it was over.

On the walls hung portraits, each by the most celebrated artist of the day, of Miss Penelope Amelia Diana 'Benkers' Benkinsop's predecessors as owners of the magnificent Georgian mansion. From Regency, through Victorian, Edwardian and World War I to the present incumbent, there was a strong family resemblance which was inevitable. Every one bore the same name and, in fact, they were all her ancestors. Each was illustrated wearing the height of the period's formal fashion and all, even the one posed against a background of what was clearly a hunting camp in the open range country of the United States of America during the mid-1870s,[2] had on the splendid diamond, sapphire and emerald necklace which – having been recovered by Amanda, Penny and herself, along with the rest of her jewellery stolen at the misguided instigation of the now deceased leading member of the Mediterranean Syndicate –[3] had graced her neck the night before.

'Good morning, ma'am,' Amanda greeted and, discov-

2. The scene is a stylized representation from the visit paid by that generation's Miss Amelia Penelope Diana 'Benkers' Benkinsop to the United States, some details of which are recorded in: BEGUINAGE IS DEAD!; Part Three, 'Birds Of A Feather', WANTED! BELLE STARR *and* Part Five, 'The Butcher's Fiery End', J.T.'S LADIES.

3. Told in: BLONDE GENIUS.

3a. Having been out of print for some considerable time, this is the rarest of our titles and much sought after by dedicated readers. Six copies which have passed through the hands of the J.T. EDSON APPRECIATION SOCIETY *to be auctioned to members for charity have fetched, £60.00, US$ 75.00, US$ 60.00, £30.00 and two at £25.00 apiece. Not bad for a paperback book which only cost thirty pence when published in 1973.*

ering the Headmistress was not alone she added 'Good morning, Miss Frithington-Babcock.'

'Good morning, my –um – dear,' replied the Deputy Headmistress, peering somewhat vaguely at the girl over a pince-nez which she always wore so far down her nose that it was practically useless as an aid to vision, yet with the warmth and affection she displayed to all the pupils even when catching them out in some misdemeanour. As usual when not actively engaged in something demanding more concentration than discussing the events of the previous evening with her superior, such as indulging in her hobby of cultivating rare species of mushrooms, she was shuffling a pack of cards then cutting and nullifying the cut with a deft finesse and precision a professional magician, or a card sharp, would have envied if he had been able to detect her doing it. 'I trust you aren't–um–working too hard?'

Tall, white haired and slender, Miss Hortense Frithington-Babcock, G.M., C.M.G.,[4] invariably had a slightly bemused expression which was *very* misleading on her still handsome, albeit pallid, features. She was dressed after a fashion which tended to emphasise her advanced age and connections with the grand old days of Great – as it was *then* – Britain's colonial empire and influence throughout the rest of the world. It was not generally known, but the employment of the totally unnecessary pince-nez and slight hesitancy when speaking were in memory of a close and *very* friendly association with the now deceased prominent detective, Mr Jeremiah Golden

4. G.M.; 'George Medal', the highest award for courage and selfless devotion to the country given to British civilians. C.M.G.; Companion of the Order of St. Michael and St. George, sometimes flippantly known as the 'Colonial Made Gentleman' because it was frequently awarded to members of the Civil Service operating overseas throughout the British Empire. Miss Hortense Frithington-Babcock received both hers for services in Counter Intelligence during World War II.

Reeder.[5] There was, however, no foundation in the Third Form rumour that 'Frithy-Bab' – as she was known behind her back, or so they believed, to the pupils – was in attendance when the first Miss Benkinsop danced "deucedly undraped" before the Prince Regent and Beau Brummel to such effect that the mansion was presented to her by the royal spectator.

'No, ma'am,' the School Swot responded to what was the invariable greeting from the well liked and respected "Frithy-Bab". 'All I've done this morning is call at the San to see Penny and Cook.'

'How are they – um – both?' Miss Frithington-Babcock asked.

'A bit stiff and sore, ma'am, but all right otherwise,' Amanda reported, feeling sure the Headmistress had already made the same inquiry to Matron at the Sanitorium. 'And, of course, most *cross* over having let the School down so badly.'

'They don't have the slightest need to be,' Miss Benkinsop declared magnanimously. 'Everybody said it was a *magnificent* debate, in fact, the *best* we've ever had, and were asking when we can arrange a re-match. What is more, Mr Spender is so insistent that we do so, he has said he personally will greatly increase the purse – I think the term is – next time.'

'I should think he – um – would, too,' Miss Frithington-Babcock claimed, although she never attended the Debating Evenings, having too gentle a nature to watch pain and

5. *Although as yet the relationship has not been made public, some details of the career of Mr Jeremiah Golden Reeder is recorded by Edgar Wallace in:* ROOM 13, THE MIND OF MR J.G. REEDER, RED ACES, MR J.G. REEDER RETURNS *and* TERROR KEEP.

5a. *Mr Reeder's organization plays a prominent part in the events we describe in:* 'CAP' FOG, TEXAS RANGER, MEET MR J.G. REEDER *and* THE RETURN OF RAPIDO CLINT AND MR J.G. REEDER.

suffering being inflicted upon other human beings.

'I'm sorry you had to miss the Debating evening, dear?' the Headmistress apologised, it being usual for the School Swot to attend each one even though the other pupils were only accorded the privilege as a special treat.

'That's all right, ma'am,' Amanda asserted. 'I can always watch the debates on the close-circuit television's video-tapes now I've got *it* finished.'

'Then it's ready for collection?' Miss Benkinsop inquired.

'The modifications are complete,' the School Swot replied, with just a suggestion – to somebody who knew her as well as the two teachers – of the pride she felt over her efforts on a very special assignment she had been given. 'I'm *sure* it will do *everything* requested, but—!'

'Yes, dear?' the Headmistress prompted.

'I would like to give it a *trial*,' Amanda admitted. 'I know it performed to the required specifications at Brooklands on Tuesday night—!'

'It *bettered* the specifications, I'd say,' Miss Benkinsop corrected, thinking of the impressive results achieved by the School Swot in the test she had arranged to take place after the motor racing circuit at Brooklands was closed for the day to ensure it was kept a secret.

'Thank you, ma'am,' Amanda said, looking down with due modesty at the praise. 'However, I would prefer to give it a test run under the kind of conditions in which it is intended to be used.'

'Hum, you have a *point*, dear,' the Headmistress concurred. 'But I don't quite see *how* we can arrange for one. It would *hardly* be appropriate in any built up area.'

'Perhaps we could hold it on the lanes around Lower and Upper Grebe?' Amanda suggested, having given the matter some thought. 'Penny says she is willing to come along – just to act as ballast, of course.'

'I don't *doubt* Miss Parkerhouse would be willing,' Miss Benkinsop said dryly, knowing the Head Girl's zest for life and love of adventure, especially when it could be spiced with an element of danger and in the company of her best friend and frequent fellow conspirator, the School Swot.

However, before any more could be said, the blue telephone – its number being in the directory, while the other was known only to a few very carefully selected friends – buzzed and the Headmistress picked up the receiver.

'Listen, you bitch!' a husky masculine voice demanded, before the Miss Benkinsop could speak. 'You don't *know* me–!'

'Something tells me that I wouldn't *want* to know you,' the Headmistress answered in a cold tone. While speaking, she made a gesture which Miss Frithington-Babcock construed correctly and, laying aside the pack of cards, she switched on the apparatus installed by Amanda to automatically record conversations whilst at the same time playing them sufficiently loud for the other occupants of the study to hear. 'But I don't suppose *that* will stop you.'

'Don't get smart with *me*, you toffee-nosed Tory-voting bitch!' the caller snarled and, continuing to punctuate his words with gratuitous profanities, went on, 'But I've got pictures of what you call a "Debating Evening" which I'm *sure* neither you nor those two lousy screws from Lower Grebe Approved School For Girls would want putting in a newspaper.'

'I see,' Miss Benkinsop said in a milder voice, yet one like ice. As far as appearances went, she was completely unmoved by either the profanity or the information. The same applied to the Deputy Headmistress and the School Swot, although neither they nor she approved of the bad language. 'It seems I'm faced with a case of blackmail.'

CHAPTER FOUR

'Call it what you want,' snarled the man on the other end of the telephone, inserting a procreative profanity between the fifth and sixth words and continuing to do so as he elaborated, 'But you're going to buy those pictures, or they'll be in the *Times* for all your snotty-nosed Tory friends to see before the week's out.'

'I wouldn't want *that*,' Miss Benkinsop replied, although she felt sure the editor would decline to use the photographs when she appraised him of the reason for their offer. However, she was equally aware there were newspapers with lower standards of ethics which would jump at the opportunity. Therefore, she was concerned by the probable adverse effect their publication could have upon the careers of Ms Ann Dulverton and Ms Stephanie Thorpe – who had only consented to appear as contenders in the Debating Evening as a gesture of respect to her and to help augment their inadequate salaries as wardresses at Lower Grebe A.S.G. 'But I will expect *complete* proof that I am buying *all* of them and the negatives before I hand over a penny.'

'You'll have what I want to give you,' the caller replied.

'That's not *good* enough,' the Headmistress stated, satisfied the attempt to sound menacing was more bluster than actual. It was no more convincing than the Cockney accent he was employing. 'While I'm willing to pay *once*, merely to avoid inconvenience, I've no intention of allowing you to keep threatening me and I will put the matter in the hands of Big Maxie Spender if you try.' Hearing a gasp which suggested the man had not considered such an unpleasant and alarming contingency, she expanded on the point, 'I'm *sure* he will be able to find out who you are and, as you undoubtedly know, regardless of what might eventuate to myself and the two ladies you mentioned, your health will be too seriously impaired for the money to be of any benefit whatsoever to you, other than to pay your hospital bills when that happens.'

'Big Maxie don't *scare* me—!' the blackmailer

began, but his voice lacked conviction.

'Then I may as well call him right now,' Miss Benkinsop countered.

'Don't do *that*!' the caller said, but the words were closer to a request than a demand. 'Provided I get five thousand quid, you'll have *everything* and won't be hearing from me again.'

'That *sounds* satisfactory,' the Headmistress conceded. 'How and where do we make the exchange?'

'I'll let you know when I've th—when I'm good and ready,' the man replied and the line went dead.

'If there is *one* – um – thing I cannot *abide*', Miss Hortense Frithington-Babcock declared with what for her was very unusual vehemence, as the Headmistress replaced the receiver, 'It's a – um – blackmailer!' Even in such worrying circumstances, the habit of appearing vague, hesitant and unworldly did not leave her. Rather it was intensified and served, as it had with Mr Jeremiah Golden Reeder, to sharpen her faculties ready for whatever lay ahead.

'I *agree*!' Miss Benkinsop concurred.

'I feel the same way,' Amanda Tweedle stated, looking like a perplexed and distressed pixie. However, while possessing sufficient good manners not to contradict her elders, she proved there was something more than this behind her contribution to what she knew was not merely a register of objections to blackmail. She was well aware that neither teacher had the kind of spirit which would submit to such treatment, or even consider placing it in the hands of outsiders. She knew they were thinking of how to cope themselves and she wanted to do everything she could to help. 'But it's the *photographs* part which worries me most. I just *knew* I should have put together and installed another film-fogging beam.'

'Don't castigate yourself, my dear,' the Headmistress instructed gently, despite the most disturbing information she had received. She never forgot her responsibility was to prevent her pupils from feeling despondent when things went wrong. '*Nobody* could have assumed it would be *necessary* in the gym during a Debating Evening, or anywhere else on the premises. After all, it *never* has been and the other was *badly* needed by the Monday Club since that left wing gutter-rag was given one of the K.G.B's concealable spy-cameras for its services to Russia and has been keeping its members under surveillance in the hope of finding something to discredit them.'

'But *who* would have done such a – um – thing?' the Deputy Headmistress inquired. 'I'd *hate* to think it was one of our – um – parents, but nobody else was – um – invited.'

'Not *invited* as you mean, Hortense,' Miss Benkinsop admitted, remembering one of the conversations she had had with Maxwell Spender during the tag team debate the previous evening. 'Would you put the video-tape of the audience in, please, Amanda?'

'Yes, ma'am,' the School Swot assented.

Going to the mahogany cabinet under the portrait of that generation's Miss Benkinsop during her visit to the United States, Amanda opened it to display a television set and one of the video recorders which were being made available to the public. Switching both on and waiting a few seconds for them to warm up, she inserted the appropriate video-tape. Setting it into motion manually, she picked up the remote control device she had developed when the machine arrived – as such things were not yet made commercially for use with the still far from frequently seen equipment – and returned to stand demurely behind the teachers.

'See if you can pick *him* out, dear,' Miss Benkinsop requested, as a scene of the audience in the gymnasium came into view.

'Yes, ma'am,' Amanda replied, refraining from handing over the control as she knew she was expected to use it instead of either teacher.

'I *never* expected we would have to do *this*, Hortense,' the Headmistress claimed in a mixture of remorse and annoyance, watching the way in which the camera – which was concealed in a room over the gymnasium – had been directed along each row of chairs so the occupants could be clearly seen.

'Nobody – um – else would have either, Amelia,' the

Deputy Headmistress said soothingly. 'But dear Amanda was *so* eager to instal the – um – camera, it wouldn't have been kind to stop her and we *always* clean off the – um – pictures as soon as possible.'

Because the seating arrangements were based upon how Miss Benkinsop regarded the standing of each invited guest within the various levels of criminal activity, she was relieved when there was no comment from the School Swot while the first three rows were under examination. Possessing pride in her judgement of character, she would have disliked finding it was incorrect; as had proved the case with the now deceased head of the Mediterranean Syndicate.

'I would *guess* it is *him*,' Amanda assessed, pressing the switch of the control which halted the advance of the tape and obtained a clarity of "still" picture the commercial devices of that kind would only rarely attain when they came on to the market.

'I know Mr – um – Pearman wouldn't hestitate to dabble in – um – blackmail, Amelia' Miss Frithington-Babcock said dubiously, wondering whether the School Swot was for once making an error of judgement. She appeared more decisive than usual as she went on, 'But I also wouldn't have imagined he had sufficient – um – intelligence to do it. Or the – um – courage, after what happened to that *nasty* – er – *gentleman* – from Cyprus who instigated the theft of your jewellery.'

'I don't mean Mr Pearman, if you please, ma'am,' Amanda contradicted politely. Continuing to show her distaste for having to contradict an elder, especially one as well liked as "Frithy-Bab", she went on, 'Unless I'm mistaken, that *person* next to him is responsible.'

'So I suspected,' Miss Benkinsop confirmed, having remembered what she heard about the occupation of the unprepossessing young man seated next to John Pearman and added it to her knowledge of the present given by the Russians to the *Daily Twinkle*. 'Although we weren't introduced, thank goodness, Maxwell told me that he's the television critic for one of those left wing gutter-rags.'

'He certainly *looks* the – um – type who'd do something like it and make such a – um – telephone call,' Miss Frithington-Babcock decided. 'His kind always seem to have an obsession with using – um – profanity. It must be some kind of ego-trip – I think the modern – um – term is – to make them believe they are lowering the level of their conversation to that of the – um – working class. There's only one thing, though. Would he be able to take photographs suitable for publication from where he was sitting?

'He would, provided the Russians have duplicated the specimen of the camera I developed two years ago for Sir M—!' the School Swot began.

'For *Mailed-Fist*, dear,' Miss Benkinsop interrupted, being a stickler for the proprieties, even though she knew the other two were aware of the identity and the position as head of the British Secret Service held by the man in question.

'Yes, ma'am,' Amanda replied with contrition. 'We know that, after it was put into service, the Russians were presented with an example by one of Her Majesty's supposedly loyal Civil Servants at the Ministry of Defence. If they duplicated the mechanism and lens, which I assume they have the facilities to do, it would give him the pictures he needed no matter how lacking in skill he probably is.'

'Then we must assume he was using the *Daily Twinkle's* camera, perhaps without the editor's knowledge and permission,' the Headmistress stated, remembering she had told the School Swot of the theft and, later, the destination of one such camera which was returned to England. 'And decide what we are going to do about him.'

'I could go and get the photographs and negatives tonight from wherever he lives,' Amanda suggested, knowing that obtaining the piece of information would be the easiest part of the task.

'That would be the *best* solution,' Miss Benkinsop agreed, after having made two telephone calls. The first produced the address and the other pertinent details about the building in which Charles Tremayne had an apartment. In the second instance, she was informed that the television critic would almost certainly be attending a party given by a left wing Socialist Member of Parliament at what was termed a "gay" club, and would be expected to be away until at least the early hours of the morning. Then she gave a cluck signifying annoyance. 'But Colonel and Lady Stapleford are coming to dinner this evening and they specifically asked for you to be present.'

'Perhaps I could go after we've eaten?' Amanda hinted. 'With the schedule I hope to carry out, they would supply me with an alibi should one be needed.'

'I hope it doesn't come to *that*,' the Headmistress answered, although she approved of the precaution in principle. 'But no matter how tight a schedule you plan to follow, it will make the expedition rather a *late* night for you.'

'Not if I use the trip to give the car a road trial,' Amanda countered, with what some people might have considered to be guileless innocence; although it did not strike either of her small audience in such a light. 'I'm *sure* Penny will be feeling up to coming along and lending me whatever assistance I might need.'

'And I'm *sure* she will *say* she is, whether that is true or not,' Miss Benkinsop said with a smile. Then, after an amused glance at the Deputy Headmistress, she went on, 'Very well. Provided Matron says it's all right for Penelope to go along, you can do it *your* way, dear.'

'Thank you, ma'am,' the School Swot replied. 'I'd better go and check that the car and everything I might need is ready.'

'She's taking no chances on me changing my mind,' the Headmistress remarked, after Amanda left more hurriedly than was decorous or usual. 'Tell me Hortense, who *won* on that business of giving the car for Mailed-Fist a road trial?'

'Let me – um – put it *this* way, Amelia,' Miss Frithington-Babcock replied. 'I wouldn't say you – um – *lost*, but you definitely came – um – *second*.'

CHAPTER FIVE

'Cor, "Mand", you aren't half clever,' Penelope Parkerhouse praised in her pronounced Cockney accent. The time was half past six in the evening and she had not long arrived from the Sanatorium. Wearing only a black lace bra and briefs worthy of the designation, which showed her curvaceously close to buxom little figure to its best advantage, she was standing by her bed and alternatively raising above her head the eight pound dumbbells she was holding in her hands. Without the vigorous exercise in anyway impeding her speech, she elaborated, 'I just fancied a run up to the Smoke in that car you've been working on and you've been and gone and fixed it up with Benkers.'

'I'm afraid it won't be much of a trip,' Amanda Tweedle warned, looking up from the map she had been studying and correlating with certain other relevant information regarding Charles Tremayne's apartment. It had all been delivered from London half an hour earlier, in response to the request Miss Benkinsop had made to a source specializing in the supply of such details. 'Not like the time we were allowed to go and deal with that little problem for Mr Spender at his Puppydog Club.'[1]

'I didn't think it would,' the Head Girl said, a trifle wistfully. 'But it'll be *better* thanjust sitting around in the San.'

'You're sure you feel up to going, though, dear?' the School Swot inquired with genuine concern for her best friend's welfare.

'Blimey, yes!' Penny declared, putting down the dumbbells. She glanced at her shapely body, its bronzed skin marred by the bruises acquired during the tag team debate, and grinned. However, her tone was still wistful as she continued, 'It's not as if I'll have to do *anything* 'cept sit in the car while you make the climb and get the stuff out of his safe. Will it be *hard*?'

The conversation was taking place in the fair-sized

1. Told in: Part One, 'Fifteen The Hard Way', J.T.'S LADIES.

room on the third floor which was allocated to the girls as a privilege granted by their standing in the heirarchy of the school. It was comfortably furnished with two beds and wardrobes, a dressing-table, a sideboard, a well filled bookcase, a dining table and four chairs. There were items such as the weights and devices for strengthening the hands' grip and wrestling magazines lying amongst technical journals covering various subjects, indicating the diverse interests of the occupants.

'I think I'll be able to do it, given a bit of *luck*,' Amanda asserted with becoming modesty. While speaking, she watched her friend tiptoeing in a circuitous route across the room and, guessing why this was happening, she continued in a louder voice, 'I hope that the re-match everybody is asking for eventuates.'

'And me!' the Head Girl seconded in a normal tone, but it rose as she jerked open the door and lunged through saying, '*Gotcha*!'

A startled and pain-filled yelp, accompanied by a tinkle as if some small item made of glass had been dropped and broken, came from the passage into which Penny disappeared. When she returned a moment later, she was dragging an almost angelically pretty blonde girl – who was in the Third Form, an inch smaller and some years younger than herself – by the ear with her right thumb and forefinger.

'All right, Vi Suggett,' the Head Girl snapped, kicking the door closed and releasing her hold. 'What's the bleeding game, hey?'

'I – I – I –!' the Third Former gasped. Then the confusion left her face and, adopting an expression so redolent of innocence she might have been speaking the truth, she went on, 'I've come to see if Amanda wants anything.'

'Pull the other one, it's got bells on it,' Penny said coldly, although the excuse was reasonable as the youngster was the School Swot's fag. 'When I opened the door, you'd got your eye to the keyhole and a glass in your hand that I bet you'd been using to listen to us, like you was casing the joint.'

'*Really* Violet!' Amanda said in mild exasperation.

'Surely you've been taught *better* than to let yourself be caught out so easily?'

'It was what you was saying about the bloke putting the black on Benkers that made me careless,' the Third Former claimed in exculpation, blushing at the thought of having earned a rebuke from the person who ranked next to the Headmistress and "Frithy-Bab" in her esteem. 'The bleeder—!'

'*Language*, Violet!' the School Swot warned, looking like a pixie in a stern mood. 'You're not some middle class-middle management left wing non-entity trying to use such talk to prove to the "workers" you're on their side because you're willing to lower yourself to talking as you believe they do.'

''Mand's *right*, like *always*, luv,' Penny seconded, although she occasionally employed the same term in the heat of the moment. 'You wait until you get into the Sixth Form before you start saying things like "bleeder", or you'll find yourself writing, "I mustn't use swear-words" five hundred times.'

'I'm *sorry*, Amanda, Penelope!' Violet Suggett apologised with genuine contrition. 'But *he* deserves *more* than just to have you take those pictures and negatives out of his safe after what he's done to Benkers.'

'You have been wigging on us for a *long* time,' Penny said. Realizing the reason must have been overheard as well as the measures Amanda had told her they would take to counter the threatened blackmail, she continued with indignation, 'You cheeky little blee—*girl*, I'll—!'

'I was just going to *knock* and ask if I could come with you,' Violet claimed, watching the clearly irate Head Girl and ready to take evasive action if some form of summary punishment such as a "clip on the ear" was directed her way.

'*You*?' Penny almost yelped.

'Amanda's taught me to handle locks almost as good as she can,' the Third Former pointed out. 'And *you* haven't ever been any good in the Household Hint class.'

'Since when's "Mand" *ever* needed any *help* to do *anything*?' Penny challenged, although she was honest enough to know she could not refute the assertion regarding her lack of ability in that particular specialized subject of the School's extra-educational curriculum.[2]

'Really, Penny, you do *exaggerate*!' Amanda protested, albeit in her usual mild fashion, finding, as was frequently the case, that the complete faith in her abilities invariably expressed by her best friend was somewhat embarrassing. 'I've *often* needed help!'

'And you *might* tonight,' Violet pointed out. 'And, if you asked for volunteers, *everybody* would want to come with you. They're *all* going to get the dead needle when they hear what's happened and you didn't give them a chance.'

'It's better that *nobody* hears what's happened, or *why*,' Amanda declared, eyeing her fag in a warning fashion.

'I *know*,' the Third Former admitted and, although she had no intention of doing so, she went on in what she hoped was a disarming fashion, 'But I *might* let something slip out if I *have* to stay here and get asked where you are.'

'You won't if you're locked in a bleeding cupboard until we get back!' Penny threatened, despite admiring the youngster's spirit and determination to be included on the expedition.

2. As we explain in BLONDE GENIUS, *in addition to providing excellent tuition for the conventional educational studies, Benkinsop's Academy For The Daughters Of Gentlefolk also instructed the pupils in various types of enterprize which might be of use to them when they left. The 'Folk Dancing' Class catered for those with suitable appearances who wished to become engaged in 'striptease', 'fan', or other forms of exotic dancing. Girls who lacked the physical attributes necessary for 'folk dancing', or who planned to embark upon the careers followed by their respective families, could attend: 'Household Hints', for various techniques of lock picking and safe-breaking; 'Wise Shopping', to learn the art of being a 'hoister', known in less well informed circles as a 'shop-lifter'; 'American Customs', imparting knowledge of all forms of gambling, fair and cheating; 'Art Appreciation', including counterfeiting as well as forging paintings and hand-writing; or 'Practical Pleasantries', supplying lessons in the performance of various confidence tricks.*

'And she'd be out before you'd turned away, even if you stripped her naked – which I know you wouldn't,' the School Swot asserted, knowing the Third Former to have a first class knowledge and ability at all aspects of the Household Hints Class which was part in hereditary – both sides of her family having been experts in that line of criminal endeavour for generations – and as a result of expert tuition from the instructors brought in by Miss Benkinsop. Then she gave a smile, 'Very well, Violet. You can come with us.'

'Oh goody!' the Third Former enthused. 'When do we start?'

'At half past eight, the dinner I have to attend will be over by then and Benkers will make sure I'm not asked to stay for long,' Amanda replied. 'The school's uniform is hardly appropriate for our purpose, Violet, so pick out a suitable disguise and meet us here at twenty past.'

* * *

'Why you cheeky little *perisher*!' Penny Parkerhouse ejaculated, staring at the Third Former as she entered the room at the appointed time. 'If I thought you was taking the mickey—!'

'Who *me*?' Violet Suggett replied. Everything about her demeanour suggested such an idea had never occurred to her, even though she often employed the attire she had on to amuse her classmates by impersonating the Head Girl. 'I just thought *nobody* would guess I came from *here* with me looking like *this*.'

'I'm *sure* they *won't*,' Amanda Tweedle said with a smile, removing the demure and yet most attractive long sleeved dress she had worn while attending the dinner with Miss Benkinsop and the distinguished guests. 'Or *you*, if it comes to *that*, Penny.'

The appearances presented by the Head Girl and the Third Former indicated there was justification for the School Swot's assertion.

In fact, regardless of the disparity in their ages, the other two girls looked remarkably alike. Each was wearing a brown soft leather windcheater with its front open to show a *very* well filled white 'tanktop' blouse inscribed, 'TINY BUT TOUGH', equally figure hugging black matador pants and white ankle socks ending in heel-less black pumps. The resemblance was increased by Violet having her own hair concealed beneath a realistic wig which duplicated Penny's tightly curled and piled up blonde locks. In the case of the Head Girl, the sizeable rounded mounds forced against the thin white material of her 'tanktop' caused the nipples to stand out in bold relief. It was firm flesh and the same applied to the contours set off by the rest of the attire. However, being younger and, therefore, not so well developed physically, those of the Third Former had been produced by extremely natural looking padding and deliberately gave the impression that she was even more adequately endowed in the bosom.

Removing the dress, Amanda proved to be clad in a flesh coloured nylon body stocking which established she was equally as shapely – if not quite so prominently endowed – as her best friend and corresponded to every curve of her body in such a way she gave the impression of being naked. She partially covered it beneath a sleeveless blue and white candy-striped mini-dress which had a décolleté so extreme she would not have thought of appearing in public clad in such an immodest fashion without the impulsion of extremely serious and urgent motivation. The footwear she put on was the same as her companions. However, although appearing no more than decorative, the red leather belt she buckled about her trim waist contained all the tools she anticipated needing for the foray.

Making sure they were unobserved, the trio left the room and hurried downstairs. Still taking successful precautions against being seen, they made their way to the garage. Inside, looking plebian and out of place in the company of Miss Benkinsop's Rolls Royce and Jaguar, was what appeared to be an ordinary brown family car of the kind to be seen in hundreds of thousands on the roads of the British Isles and the Continent. Either the 'Roller' or the 'Jag' would have struck most people as offering the kind of speed necessary to maintain the schedule Amanda planned to follow in the interests of avoiding an over-late night and to provide an alibi should one be needed, but they did not go to them. Instead, they boarded the other vehicle. Shortly after Amanda had driven the car through the magnificent wrought iron gates of the School, the reason for the selection was soon made apparent.

At the request of 'Mailed-Fist', the School Swot had carried out certain modifications to the family car which would equip it for the needs of one of his operatives bearing the rare 'license to kill' designation. Being less boyant by nature than the senior member of the three-man squad, the operative had requested a vehicle which – while having certain specialized facilities and the capability of very high speeds and manoeuvrability of an exceptional order – would be able to pass unnoticed instead of the eye-catching Aston-Martin or other 'up-market' types of car favoured by his associate.

Receiving the selected car, in adding to other specialized fittings, Amanda had worked on the improved type of engine with which it had been fitted to gain an even greater potency where speed and strength was concerned. She had also ensured its steering, brakes and other fitments were capable of coping with the improvements. Despite the modifications having proved satisfactory during the trial she had carried out at Brooklands race track, Amanda was eager to put the car to a test on ordinary roads and in much the kind of conditions for which it was envisaged.

The blackmail threat had presented the School Swot with an opportunity and she was meaning to make the most of it!

CHAPTER SIX

'Blimey, what a *swizz*!' Penelope Parkerhouse protested, as the car was reversed into position and brought to a halt on the parking lot of the apartment building where Charles Tremayne was living. 'After all the work you've done on this thing, I thought we'd have a bit of *excitement* coming here. I don't like to complain, "Mand", but you drove as careful as my Aunt Mabel.'

'But a trifle more slowly, I hope,' Amanda Tweedle replied with a smile, knowing the relative mentioned by the Head Girl was not only the daughter of the celebrated Henry 'Harry The Jump-Up' Fredericks,[1] but also highly thought of in her own right as a driver of getaway vehicles for the South London and Southern England Crime Consortium. 'There wasn't any need for me to go faster and I didn't want to arouse unwanted interest by doing so.'

'I suppose you're *right*,' Penny sighed wistfully. 'No matter what you say, you *always* are.'

Instead of the School Swot having utilized the full potential for speed she had imparted to the vehicle, as the Head Girl and implied, the journey from the School to London had been made at the legitimate speed for each type of road and location and without incident. On reaching the suburbs, her well developed knowledge of the

1. Information about the career of Henry 'Harry The Jump-Up' Fredericks can be found in: 'Ace Of Jump-Ups', UNDERWORLD NIGHTS, *by Charles Raven. Hulton Press, 1956.*

1a. How Henry's father, Albert Henry 'Bert The Jump-Up' Fredericks met his end is told in: 'CAP' FOG, TEXAS RANGER, MEET MR J.G. REEDER.

1b. The sobriquet arose from and was handed down through several earlier generations of the Fredericks' family due to its members specializing in waiting in suitable attire outside public houses or other places until a carrier left his horse-drawn vehicle unattended, then climbing – 'jumping' – aboard and driving it away. Since the coming of motor cars, they had also developed considerable skill in driving getaway vehicles.

city's geography had enabled her to make a more active contribution to the mission by acting as guide to their ultimate destination. However, having studied the most recent maps, Amanda had warned that at one point they would have to take a different route than was given to avoid a 'one-way' system which had not been in existence the last time the Head Girl has passed through the area.

Approaching the apartment building along an almost deserted street, Amanda had scrutinized its architecture carefully and mentally compared what she saw with the plans and other information she had studied before setting out. By the time she was turning into the partially filled parking lot, she was satisfied that the source from which the details had come was accurate. The building was modern in design, twelve stories high and with each successive apartment having a bay window opening on to a small balcony in a way which formed a series of evenly spaced oblong protuberances along the frontage.

While speaking to her best friend, having turned the bonnet of the vehicle outwards to facilitate a hurried departure should one be required, Amanda continued her examination. Due to the stone-throwing proclivities of the local youngsters and the disinclination of the building's maintenance staff to keep effecting repairs which would be broken by the next evening, there were only a couple of lights working in the parking lot and she was able to stop in the shadows without needing to worry about the vehicle being made more noticeable. What was more, the few patches of illumination from the windows of the apartments tended to emphasise rather than decrease the shadows thrown by the angles of the protruding walls. Except for the difficulty involved in making the climb to the television critic's apartment on the third floor,[2] which

2. We are using the English system of numbering the stories of a building, which commences with the 'ground' floor and then 'first', 'second', etc.; whereas Americans start with the 'first' and count up from there.

she was confident she and Violet Suggett could overcome, she regarded the conditions as suitable for their purpose as the information had indicated. Not that the first aspect had been played down in any way by the report. It had warned that trouble expected in the ascent had deterred several men who specialized in making climbs up the sides of buildings as a means of obtaining access to carry out a burglary.

'Well, time's going by and we've a schedule to try and keep,' the School Swot said, opening the driver's door and getting out. 'Let's get started, Violet.'

'You two are going to have all the *fun*,' Penny protested *sotto voce*, as she and the Third Former joined the School Swot.

'And *you* have all the *fun* on Debating Evenings,' Amanda countered, knowing the protest was made as an aid to relieving the concern her best friend was feeling for herself and her fag over what lay ahead.

'That's *your* fault for being so *good* Benkers can't put you up against *anybody*, 'cause they wouldn't have a *chance*,' the Head Girl pointed out with a grin. Then she looked around and continued hopefully, 'Maybe some yobbo will come around to try and nick the car while you're gone.'

'Don't be *too* rough with him if one does,' the School Swot replied, also smiling in a way which made her resemble an unconventionally dressed but happy fairy on a Christmas tree. 'Are you ready, Violet?'

'Yes,' the Third Former assented, having taken off and deposited her windcheater in the back of the car.

Going with the other girls to the side of the building, Penny looked up and felt a sense of perturbation. Despite the faith she always expressed in Amanda's ability to cope with any and every situation, she felt decidedly uneasy as she gazed upwards over what seemed to her to be a sheer and smooth wall. It would be hard enough for even the School Swot to surmount, but the task would be far more difficult for the smaller Third Former, regardless of the instruction she had received at the Household Hints Class where this essential part of the house-breaking business was concerned. In fact, the Head Girl knew going 'on the climb' was so specialized an undertaking that only a few of those attending the Class studied its requirements and the failure rate amongst them was high. She took comfort from remembering that, in addition to having received the kind of superlative teaching in subjects pertaining to the 'Redistribution Industry' for which Benkinsop's Academy For The Daughters Of Gentlefolk was justifiably famous, Violet was following in the tradition established by the Suggett family over many generations and was considered the member of the Class most likely to achieve success.

While aware of the dangers of over-confidence, the Third Former was experiencing less concern over the climb than the Head Girl. Not only had she been taught well by her father and the instructors supplied by Miss Benkinsop, she had also received much practical advice from the School Swot. However, as they were making the preliminaries for the ascent, a problem arose which had never been envisaged by anybody concerned with running the Household Hints Class or even Amanda.

Having flexed her very powerful fingers, selecting the cracks between the bricks and any small protuberances on the surfaces as hand- and foot-holds, the School Swot had started to climb the wall. However, when duplicating her action of pressing against the wall as the first step in following, Violet found it impossible to accomplish. Although the School Swot had grown accustomed to working with such genuine appendages to a well developed feminine physique, the Third Former found herself seriously impeded by the mounds of padding required to simulate the extremely prominent bosom for her impersonation of the Head Girl.

'What's *up*?' Penny inquired.

'My bleeding "falsie's" in the way!' Violet replied, turning around.

'*Blimey*!' the Head Girl ejaculated, staring at the Third

Former and, instead of delivering a rebuke for the use of profanity, she instinctively touched the region of her own body which was causing the problem. 'They don't *never* give me no *trouble*. 'Course, I don't go on the climb neither.' Then she shrugged and continued in a helpful tone, 'There's only one thing for it. You'll have to take them off!'

'They're stitched into the tank-top too firm to get them out,' Violet replied, sounding close to tears. 'And I haven't got *anything* else on under it.'

'Bloody hell!' Penny gasped, considering the unanticipated development called for a strength of profanity which would not have met with the approval of Miss Benkinsop. 'You've got to have the bleeder on so's you can come down the stairs to get out.' Once again she paused, then declared with the air of having solved the dilemma, 'There's only one thing to do!'

'What's that?' the Third Former asked, sounding hopeful and eager to try any solution she was offered as she could not think of one herself and had no wish to delay the School Swot's carefully thought out schedule.

'Put the bloody thing on back to front,' the Head Girl instructed. 'It'll look *funny* as hell, but nobody except *me's* going to see you while you're making the climb and you can change it 'round when you get inside his flat.'

Taking the advice, although the effect was somewhat peculiar in that it gave her the appearance of a rather well rounded hunchback, Violet found she was able to follow Amanda up the wall with the same facility she had frequently shown in test projects for the Household Hints Class. Nor did she encounter any particular difficulty until, having passed the level of the first floor, the reaching fingers of her right hand failed to locate anywhere upon which they could obtain a purchase.

'I—I'm *stuck*, Amanda!' the Third Former gasped, returning the hand to its last position and concentrating upon keeping it there.

'Yes, I thought you might be,' came the cool voice of the

School Swot, having estimated the distance would prove too much for the shorter arms of her fag to cope with. She was already taking the requisite action by moving downwards a little and, easing her left foot from the crack between two bricks it was using, she lowered it.

'Get hold of my ankle, dear.'

Moving slowly and looking upwards, Violet discovered with a sensation of relief that her vision was sufficiently adapted to the gloom to be able to locate the lowered limb. Having complete faith in Amanda, she did not hesitate before acting upon the advice. Grasping the lowered ankle with first the right and then the left hand, she sought to ensure her toes helped give support to what she knew was coming. After a couple of seconds, just as she anticipated, she felt herself being drawn slowly higher until told – in a voice which hinted at the tremendous strain to which the School Swot's carefully developed physical strength and great expertise was being subjected – to release her hold with the right fingers and feel for the support now brought within her reaching distance. As she knew it would be, the next point was available to her questing hand and she was able to continue climbing.

Watching from below, Penny was just able to make out the figures of her schoolmates as blacker blobs against the light coloured bricks which were in the shadow thrown by the projections of the apartments' out-thrust balconies on either side. Such was their steady upwards progression, even with the problem they had just overcome, she formed the impression of two flies constantly crawling higher and higher. However, after a few seconds, her attention was drawn by a movement elsewhere. Looking around, she saw a young uniformed police constable walking along the pavement beyond the wall of the parking lot. Instinct caused her to move towards him and she came into his view just as he reached the entrance. This was one part of the area which still had illumination and, dressed as she was, she could see he found her appearance was well worth examination.

'Hello, love,' the Head Girl greeted, forcing her tone to be warm and friendly. Much to her satisfaction, a quick glance assured her that the shadows thrown by the protruding walls was obscuring her friends at that angle. 'Can you tell me the best way to get to the Beeb's studio at Shepherd's Bush?'

'Yes,' the constable replied, feasting his gaze upon the well defined physical attractions displayed by Penny's attire. As the apartment building was occupied by a number of people involved in the entertainment industry, he saw nothing unusual in her appearance or apparent desire to learn how to reach the television studios of the British Broadcasting Company situated in the Shepherd's Bush district. Having supplied the information, he began, 'Are you in a show th—?'

The words trailed off into a startled gasp as the policeman looked upwards and towards the apartment building. Glancing away, he snapped his head around for a classic example of what was known in theatrical circles as a 'double-take'. Following the direction in which he was staring, being curious to dicover what had distracted him from continuing to study her exposed and far from overdressed figure with a far from official – yet flattering – interest, Penny felt a sensation of alarm flood through her.

By that time, Amanda and Violet had reached the level of the second floor. However, as they were passing between the protective walls of the balconies, the French windows of the apartment at the left were thrown open. It closed again almost immediately, but not before the two girls clinging to the side of the building had been bathed in the light which flooded out to illuminate the area between it and its neighbour. What was more, brief though the interim had been, every detail of their appearances – at least as far as the backs of their bodies was concerned – had been shown in bold relief against the brickwork.

'D–Did you see *that*?' the constable croaked, staring at Penny and speaking in a voice which implied he was having difficulty in believing the evidence of his eyes.

'Did I see *what*, love?' the Head Girl inquired, with an assumed innocence which had often served her very well when playing poker with attendees of the American Customs Class.

'N–*nothing*!' the policeman lied, having no wish to make himself appear foolish – particularly to such an attractive and friendly member of the opposite sex – by mentioning the sight which he now believed to be nothing more than an over-active imagination. 'Well, not *nothing* exactly.'

'What then?' Penny asked, having taken a liking to the clean cut and wholesome appearance of the constable and hoping she would not be compelled to prevent him investigating what the light had brought into view by rendering him unconscious.

'I – I thought I saw somebody I've seen on the telly up there,' the constable claimed, producing what he believed was a passable excuse.

'It could have been,' the Head Girl asserted, with an aura of speaking the truth. 'There's a lot of 'em get around here.'

'Yes, I suppose so,' the policeman admitted. 'Well, I'd better not be delaying you any longer, miss. I hope everything goes off all right for you at the Beeb.'

'Thanks, love,' Penny replied and, as the young man resumed walking his beat, she let out a sigh of relief. 'Whoo, that was bleeding *close*!'

The Head Girl would have had no cause to revise her opinion if she had been present when, about threequarters of an hour later, the young officer had a meeting with his sergeant.

'I reckon this night beat's getting on my nerves, serge,' the constable remarked, after giving the traditional Metropolitan Police response of, 'All correct'. 'You'll *never* believe what I *thought* I saw back there.'

'Then you'd better tell me,' the sergeant advised.

'I *thought* I saw a girl in a mini-dress climbing up the wall level to the second floor of one of those high-rise apartment buildings,' the constable obliged. 'But it was only my imagination.'

'Are you *sure* of that?' the sergeant growled, although he had no doubt the assumption was correct.

'Well,' the constable said, looking worried. 'I might not have been if it wasn't for the other one I *thought* I saw just below her!'

'The *other* one?' the sergeant repeated. 'There was *two* of them?'

'Yes, except there *wasn't* any!'

'What the hell are you talking about, lad?'

'I might have believed I saw the one in the mini-dress,' the constable asserted. 'Unlikely as it was—!'

'Go on, lad,' the sergeant prompted in a not unkindly tone, being aware of the pressures faced in their daily duties by young police officers in addition to coping with the continuous smear campaigns all four networks of British television ran against the forces of law and order.

'But the other one had a great big pair of tits on her *back*!' the constable obliged. 'Serge, you've got to take me off that guard at the art gallery. Looking at all those bloody weird Picasso style paintings must be starting to send me 'round the bend!'

CHAPTER SEVEN

'We had no difficulty reaching the apartment and gaining admission across the balcony, ma'am,' Amanda Tweedle reported, glancing at Penelope Parkerhouse and deciding to go along with their decision not to mention how, during the ascent, the chance opening of the French windows in an apartment on the floor below had threatened to ruin the plan. 'Or in leaving by going down in the lift and through the front entrance as we intended.'

The time was nine o'clock in the morning and, once again acceptably clad in their school uniforms, the two girls were standing in front of the Headmistress's large desk. They had been ordered to report to 'Benkers' Pad' by Miss Rita Panchez – the large and gipsyish looking Science Mistress,[1] – while at breakfast and, for more reasons than one, neither had relished the prospect. On their arrival, they had found Miss Benkinsop with Miss Hortense Frithington-Babcock in attendance and they were instructed to tell what had happened the previous evening.

'Don't think I wish to stifle your initiative, dear,' the Headmistress said. 'But why did you elect to climb the wall to get

1. Miss Rita Panchez was, in fact, a gipsy. Although her knowledge of science did not give her the qualifications for the appointment she held, which was filled by Miss Benkinsop and Amanda Tweedle, she served the very useful function of instructing the pupils in all kinds of tricks and manipulations employed on the 'fair grounds' of the British Isles and in the American equivalent, carnivals. However, as was reported in BLONDE GENIUS, *her picture was no longer to be seen on the labels of bottles which used to be sold by the School as* 'Gipsy Rita's Cold Cure'. *The concoction had been produced by Amanda while engaged upon another project in the Science Laboratory. However, the Headmistress had yielded on the grounds of wishing to avoid causing unemployment when asked by the companies producing similar, albeit less effective, potions and took it off the market. The reason for the requests was that, unlike their products, it really did cure the common cold.*

in, yet leave by using the lift and the front entrance?'

'I was warned in the information that "the doorman" would be on duty and would probably have asked too many questions if we had gone in the front entrance, ma'am,' the School Swot replied, speaking for once without considering all the ramifications of what she was saying. 'And, the way we were dressed, I felt he was sure to remember us if Mr Tremayne reported the rifling of the safe to the police and he was questioned. On the other hand, I considered he would be used to seeing young ladies he isn't acquainted with, and who had arrived before he came on duty, leaving from the apartments they've been visiting upstairs. So he wouldn't think it was unusual for us to be doing so.'

'That was *good* thinking, dear,' Miss Benkinsop praised, always a believer in giving credit where credit was due. Having noticed the slight blush which came to Amanda's cheeks when mentioning the way 'they' were dressed, she decided against prying into the nature of what she felt sure had been attire unlikely to meet with her approval. However, as she was aware the Head Girl lacked the special skills required to participate in the climbing, she was puzzled by the repeated references to 'we' and 'us'. '*Very* good, in fact.'

'And opening the safe was so easy,' the School Swot continued, just a trifle hesitantly, being all too aware she was reaching the point where questions were going to be asked which she and Penny would have preferred to be left unsaid. 'In fact, Violet did it with no trouble at all.'

'*Violet*?' Miss Benkinsop inquired, her voice taking on a timbre which caused both girls to realize they had been correct in their assumption that she would not approve of the third member of the expedition being allowed to accompany them. 'That would be Violet *Suggett*, I presume?'

'So *that* is where she – um – went,' the Deputy Headmistress put in before either of the all too obviously worried girls could reply and using the tone she always adopted when trying to extricate pupils from the consequences of misbehaviour. 'I noticed there was only some – um – carefully arranged pillows in her bed when I made the Dorm Check last night,

Amelia, but I thought she was only – um – taking advantage of Cook still being in the San to raid the – um – kitchen and didn't want to disturb the rest of the dear – um – girls to ask.'

'*Well*, Miss Parkerhouse,' Miss Benkinsop interrogated, showing no sign of being mollified by "Frithy-Bab's" intervention. '*Why*, may I ask, did *you*, the *Head Girl*, permit a member of the Third Form to go out with you at such an unseemly hour?'

'It was as much my fault as Penelope's, ma'am,' Amanda claimed, never one to shirk the responsibility for her share of any blame which might be forthcoming. 'Violet overheard us discussing the problem and how you were allowing us to deal with it and she *insisted* upon accompanying us.'

'You let a member of the Third Form *insist*?' the Headmistress asked coldly, wondering whether the discovery she had just made was causing the girls to look so crestfallen despite the positive aspects of the expedition she had so far heard of.

'She was so *insistent* we had no other choice, ma'am!' Penny asserted and, as the School Swot nodded concurrence, went on, 'If we hadn't let her come, we'd've had her and the whole Third Form coming up the Smoke after us when she told them's that rotten bleeder was trying to put the black on you. You *know* what that lot're *like*.'

'I *do*,' Miss Benkinsop admitted, making an effort to restrain the smile which struggled to break through and, for once, overlooking the Head Girl's use of the word, 'bleeder', due to the obvious stress which caused its employment in the presence of herself and the Deputy Headmistress. 'In fact, they're *almost* as bad as the Third was when you two young madams were its leading – for want of a *better* term – lights. Don't you *agree*, Miss Frithington-Babcock?'

'Only – um – *almost*,' the older teacher corrected, peering at the girls in a benevolent and even admiring fashion over her unnecessary *pince nez*. 'I think you will agree, Amelia, theirs was a – um – *vintage* year.'

'That is *one* name for it, although not *quite* the term I had in mind – and that *wasn't* a pun, Miss Parkerhouse,'

Miss Benkinsop conceded, the last part of the comment wiping away the smile which accompanied the wink directed by Penny at Amanda. 'I might add I'm still not *entirely* satisfied with the suggestion that you two young *ladies*, the Head Girl of the School and the Senior Prefect, couldn't have found some way of avoiding taking a slip of a child like Violet Suggett with you.'

'It wouldn't have been *easy*, ma'am,' Amanda claimed, as Penny looked around in a way she knew asked for her to take over the burden of the explanation. 'There isn't a lock in the whole School she couldn't open with whatever she could get her hands on and she's so well advanced at escapology that, even if you would have approved of us employing such *crude* methods, the only way we know to tie her up so she couldn't get free would be too dangerous to use.'

'Very well,' the Headmistress said with what the girls, if not Miss Frithington-Babcock, considered was a sigh of resignation. 'I'll forget the matter – *this* time.' Having rendered the judgement, she adopted a more friendly and businesslike attitude. 'Anyway, we had got as far as Violet opening the safe.'

'Yes, ma'am,' Amanda agreed and continued to look downcast. 'Although we found several photographs he was probably using to blackmail other people, judging by the amount of money it held, our negatives and photographs weren't there.'

'That *is* a setback,' Miss Benkinsop admitted, then hastened to make amends as she saw the distress on the faces of the girls increase. 'But *you* can't be held responsible in *any* way for it, my dears. What did you do next?'

'He had the negatives and photographs in a large brown envelope,' the School Swot replied. 'So I changed them for a similar number of sheets of typing paper on his desk and brought the original photos away with us.

'Where are they now?' the Headmistress asked.

'I put them through your document shredder as soon as we got back, ma'am, and burned the remains,' Amanda answered. 'It seemed the best thing to do with them.'

'It *was*,' Miss Benkinsop declared. 'You've done *well*, dear.'

'*Very* well indeed,' Miss Frithington-Babcock seconded. 'But I wonder why he was – um – treating ours different from the – um – rest?' A look of uncharacteristic anger came to her face and she went on, 'Do you think he took them to – um – show that nasty Pearman chap, Amelia?'

'I wouldn't expect so,' the Headmistress assessed. 'Much as I share your dislike for Mr Pearman, I doubt whether he would chance becoming involved in this business. Not from any moral scruples, or liking for *us*, but because he would be all too aware of what his fate would be should our parents find he had been interfering.'

'I daresay you're – um – *right*, dear,' Miss Frithington-Babcock concurred, nodding emphatically and, for once, showing not the slightest concern over the suffering which would be inflicted upon another human being as, in these circumstances, she considered it to be justifiable. 'Perhaps our film didn't come – um – out when he had it developed, if that is the correct – um – photographic term – and he was trying a – um – bluff in the hopes of getting you to pay him anyway.'

'That *is* a possibility,' Miss Benkinsop admitted. 'Although I doubt whether his kind of product from our *wonderful* State-supported universities would have the courage, or especially the intelligence, to make such an attempt. It's more likely that he hadn't been able to have the film developed and printed during business hours at that left wing gutter rag he works for, so had to collect them on the way to that loathsome party.'

'Then he might – um – have showed them around,' the Deputy Headmistress said, clearly aghast by the possibility.

'I don't think so,' Miss Benkinsop contradicted. 'His kind have such nasty and sneaky natures themselves that they believe *everybody* else to be the same. He wouldn't trust even others of this own persuasion.'

'The thing is, ma'am,' Penny commented, ever eager for the prospect of action. 'How do we go about nobbling the bleeder now?'

'*Langauge*, Penelope!' the Headmistress boomed.

'I'm *sorry*, ma'am,' Penny apologised in genuine contrition. 'It's just so blee—*blooming* annoying after all "Mand" and Vi went through and what hap—!'

'What did "*hap*—"?' Miss Benkinsop wanted to know, the words having died away and the annoyance shown by the Head Girl was replaced by an evasive expression.

'Well, ma'am,' Penny replied, knowing better than try and avoid the question when it was posed in what was referred to throughout the School as 'Benkers' you'd better tell, or *else*' tone. 'For the life of me, I don't know *why*; but the rozzers got after us on the M-4 when we was coming back.'

'The *M-4*?' the Headmistress queried, that particular Motorway not being on the most direct route between Upper Grebe and London.

'Yes, ma'am,' the Head Girl verified, looking uneasy. 'We thought – Well, I – It was all *my* idea—!'

'No more than *mine*, Penny!' Amanda protested.

'We'll leave the apportioning of culpability for the time being,' Miss Benkinsop ordered grimly and looked at the School Swot. 'Let me hear *your* version first, if you please, Miss Tweedle.'

'I thought that, particularly as we hadn't had any *success* in our primary objective, I might as well take the opportunity to give the car a run at speed,' Amanda obliged, contriving to look at her most helpless and innocent, even though she doubted whether either teacher would be as softened by it as a male audience would have been. 'And I'm afraid I must have attracted the attention of the patrol car by going a *little* in excess of the speed limit.'

'And just how "little" was that *little*, may I ask?' Miss Benkinsop said, her suspicions aroused even more.

'Well – er –!' the School Swot began hesitantly. Then she continued in a low voice. 'One hundred and fifty miles per hour, ma'am.'[2]

2. The police officers in the patrol vehicle on the M-4 Motorway never reported the chase, feeling sure nobody would believe them if they said the ordinary looking family car had proved capable of travelling so much faster than they were capable of achieving.

'And we didn't come down much below one-twenty when "Mand" turned off the M-4 to come home by all them small country roads,' Penny enthused. 'Cor, I haven't *never* seen such driving. Not even my Aunt Mabel—!'

'I don't wish to know *that*, thank you,' the Headmistress stated, although she was impressed by what she had heard and realized she could inform Mailed-Fist that the vehicle had received a thorough testing under the kind of conditions for which the car had been intended.

'Perhaps that *dreadful* young man will be frightened out of going ahead with trying to – um – blackmail you when he finds his safe had been opened and the contents of the envelope exchanged, Amelia?' Miss Frithington-Babcock suggested, feeling the subject should be diverted from the aftermath of the visit to Tremayne's apartment. 'I should imagine the – um – discovery will come as rather a – um – shock.'

Before anybody else could comment upon the point raised by the Deputy Headmistress, the discussion was brought to an end by the blue telephone ringing. Picking up the receiver, Miss Benkinsop made a wry face and switched on the amplifier as soon as she heard who was calling.

'All right, you lousy Tory-voting bitch,' Charles Tremayne snarled, still employing the blatantly false manner of speaking which he believed prevented his true identity from being suspected, and continuing to insert his gratuitous profanities. 'I said I'd let you know how I want paying and this is *it*!'

'Perhaps I could bring the money to the Puppydog Club and give it to you there?' the Headmistress suggested when the television critic did not supply any instructions, feeling certain the location would not be accepted.

'That's *Big Max Spender's* place!' Tremayne almost yelped, after what was obviously a moment's thought. 'I saw you sucking up to him while the wrestling was going on, so we're *not* meeting there.'

'How about the Lotus House Cantonese Restaurant on Great Compton Street?' the Headmistress offered, in the fulfilled expectation that her similar friendly association with its owner was known to the television critic and would render it equally unacceptable. Having suggested and had four other locations refused for the same considerations, satisfied that Tremayne had failed to give the matter of obtaining the payment any thought, she went on, 'Well I'll leave it up to *you*. As far as I'm concerned, you can meet me and get the money anywhere you choose – except *here* at the school. It would be too difficult for me to arrange protect—It wouldn't be *convenient*!'

'It's going to be *convenient*, whether it's convenient or not,' the television critic claimed, having drawn the required – albeit erroneous – conclusion from the amended objection. 'I'll be coming there with the pictures and negatives around one o'clock and you'd better have *everything* I asked for ready when I get there.'

'Don't worry,' Miss Benkinsop replied, sounding meek and frightened, although there was nothing about her demeanour to suggest this was her true frame of mind. 'As soon as you've given me the photographs and the negatives, you'll get *everything* you're asking for and you have my *word* on *that*!'

'That is – um – *strange*,' Miss Frithington-Babcock commented, as the Headmistress hung up the receiver. 'It seems he isn't – um – worried about losing the other – um – photographs and negatives.'

'Or he hasn't been back to his flat and discovered they're gone,' Miss Benkinsop guessed. Having offered the explanation – which was correct although she never found out – she looked at the other occupants of the study and went on in a grim tone, 'Now let's decide what we're going to do about Mr Tremayne.'

'I'll leave the rest of the – um – planning to *you*,' Miss Frithington-Babcock declared, coming to her feet. Despite the hesitancy in her speech, which was too deeply ingrained to be forgotten, her whole bearing was very decisive and different from her usual behaviour. 'This is a – um – situation which calls for one of my angel cakes and I'll only just have – um – time to get it ready.'

CHAPTER EIGHT

'Well, I've come!' Charles Tremayne announced unnecessarily, having entered Miss Benkinsop's study with what he thought was a bold and truculent swagger.

'So I see,' the Headmistress replied in a mild voice. Her beautiful and patrician face showed nothing of her feelings, although her instincts made her feel she wanted to evict the unwelcome visitor with one of the Debating Evening's "points of view" in which she was very well versed. 'You can hardly expect me to say I'm *pleased* to see you.'

Coming to a halt, Tremayne was satisfied that he would not be recognized by Miss Benkinsop. While he wold have preferred to have arrived looking like an ex-serviceman who was a member of the National Front, a very frequent 'baddie' figure in the type of left wing orientated plays produced by British television and about which he invariably wrote glowingly for his column in the *Daily Twinkle*, he had realized that doing so would be impossible if he was to retain his anonymity. They tended to be short haired, clean shaven and tidily dressed, conditions he never attained under normal conditions. But he needed the long brown wig and bushy false beard he had on to conceal his distinctive – as he regarded them – features. He had also sought to reduce the chance of detection and increase what he believed to be an aura of toughness still further by wearing a shabby and ragged sports jacket, a grubby white polo-necked pullover and baggy grey flannels with the legs short enough to display red and white striped socks ending in heavy 'bovver' boots.

Studying the television critic, the Headmistress concluded that only the obviously false hair and whiskers and, probably, the footwear was different from his generally unkempt 'trendy' appearance. In fact, she considered the whisker part of the disguise was an improvement as it served to hide much of his unprepossessing and stubble-cheeked face. However, she kept her thoughts to herself and contrived to give the impression of being meek and frightened by him.

'I don't give a shit whether you're pleased to see me or not,' Tremayne stated, in what he fondly imagined was a tough and commanding voice, but which differed from his usual voice only in having a blatantly pseudo working class accent imposed upon the normal smugly condescending whine which he employed when acting as a guest critic on a show which gave new talent an opportunity of being seen on television. 'Let's be having the lolly.'

'Not until I've seen the negatives and photographs,' the Headmistress replied, in a most expert blend of what seemed to be cowed and frightened awe.

'Here they are,' the television critic announced.

While speaking – in such a cornily dramatic fashion he might have been appearing in one of the British television plays he praised so fulsomely, although they bored the vast majority of the viewers – Tremayne brought an envelope from the inside left breast pocket of his jacket. The slight hesitancy while he searched in his pocket suggested to Miss Benkinsop's experienced gaze that it was not the only one there. Opening the flap, keeping beyond reaching distance, he drew out several glossy seven inch by five inch photographs and lifted them so the one on top was facing her.

Even without needing to move closer, the Headmistress could see enough to realise the photograph was a threat to the careers of the two wardresses from Lower Grebe Approved School For Girls. It was also, she grudgingly conceded, a tribute to the skilful way in which the Russian manufacturers – or, more probably some of their numerous German former Nazi technicians – had duplicated the spy camera that Amanda had developed for Mailed-Fist and which had been presented to the Russians by a left wing civil servant at the Ministry of Defence. Depicted with perfect clarity and in colour, their faces perfectly recognizable despite the differing expressions on each, Penelope Parkerhouse was applying a 'stepover toe-hold' to Ms Ann Dulverton's left leg, and Ms Stephanie Thorpe could be seen just as plainly standing beyond the ropes in the background.

'Pooh!' Miss Benkinsop sniffed, playing her role in the scheme she had arranged by providing the time required for the rest of the participants to take up their positions. 'That is just *one* and the ladies on it might be *anybody.*'

'The rest are just as *good*!' Tremayne asserted, starting to prove the claim by showing more of the equally clear examples. 'And my pap—*The Times* will find out who they really are easily enough.'

'I suppose you're right,' the Headmistress said, with what would have passed to an even more perceptive person than the television critic as being the resignation of one who knew she was completely defeated. 'Give them and the negatives to me and you can have the money.'

'I want the money before you get them,' Tremayne demanded, thrusting forward his grimy left hand with its palm upwards.

'And I *refuse* to give you the money until I have the photographs and negatives,' Miss Benkinsop countered, restricting an almost uncontrollable urge to grab the television critic by the wrist and, employing a shoulder throw, send him headfirst through the window. 'So *there*!'

'I said I'm not—!' Tremayne began.

'Why don't you put them on one side of my desk and I'll put the money on the other?' the Headmistress offered, wanting to avoid delaying the conclusion of the negotiations any longer. She was hard-pressed to conceal her amusement at having to suggest a way by which the transaction in blackmail could be conducted. 'We'll walk around and each can check everything is as stipulated. After all, I'm only a single *defenceless* woman and you're such a big, strong *man*, so you can easily take them back if the money isn't correct.'

'That's what I was just going to say we'd do,' the television critic lied, being unable to think up a better solution and considering the last point made by Miss Benkinsop was valid. Placing the photographs on the desk, he laid the strips of negatives on them and glared across it. 'There they are.'

'And here is the money,' the Headmistress answered, opening a drawer. For a moment, she thought of bringing out the fully loaded heavy calibre revolver which lay so close to her reaching hand but, deciding to go on with the plan she had made she produced instead a thick stack of banknotes. 'The payment is in fivers, but they're all used and don't have consecutive serial numbers.'

'That'll do,' Tremayne declared, realizing that when embarking upon his first essay into blackmail he had never given a thought to the ways in which the money he received might be traced. 'Shove it over here so I can count it.'

Duplicating the way in which the photographic material was pushed across the top of the desk she did the same with the pile of money and, as she and the television critic were circling around it, Miss Benkinsop was reminded of two mistrusting children engaged in making a trade. She had to employ all her self control to prevent her amusement from showing. As she had suspected during the preliminary negotiations, although the discovery made by Amanda Tweedle the previous night suggested he had gathered material which he hoped he would be able to use for that purpose, it was obvious he had lacked the opportunity – or, more likely, courage – to try blackmailing the other potential victims and lacked experience in how to carry out the transfer. However, feeling sure he would have no difficulty in terrorizing the kind of woman which his upbringing and biased political outlook had led him to assume she would be, he had made her his first target.

'Would you like this envelope to put it in?' the Headmistress inquired, having checked that the negatives were indeed for the photographs. She dropped them all into the drawer, leaving it open so as to offer unrestricted access in the unlikely event that the big revolver should be needed.

'Give it here!' Tremayne demanded, counting the banknotes and satisfying himself they were for the required amount. Tucking them into the brightly coloured airmail envelope which the Headmistress slid across the desk, he was putting it into the same breast pocket when the door of the study opened. 'Who the *hell*—?'

Suspecting he might have fallen into some kind of trap and, being as cowardly as most of his kind, the television critic was assailed by alarm. However, it died away as he saw the person who was coming across the threshold. Nobody could have presented a less disturbing sight than Miss Hortense Frithington-Babcock as she entered carrying a tray. On it was a teapot under a flower decorated cosy, two elegant bone china cups and saucers, a couple of plates from the same clearly expensive set and a third upon which stood a large piece of an exceptionally succulent looking white cake.

'It's – um – tiffin time, Miss Benk—!' the Deputy Headmistress began. Then stopping and staring at the television critic in what appeared to be consternation, sounding at her most 'upper-bracket' and dithery, she continued, 'Oh *dear.* I didn't realize you had a – um – visitor. I will bring back the – um – tray when you're alone.'

'You'll leave it here!' Tremayne commanded harshly, always – provided he was satisfied there would be no risk involved – willing to act the bully against anybody with whose political viewpoint or social background he disagreed. Swaggering across the room, he took the tray and put it on the desk. Then he grabbed up the piece of cake and went on, 'I'm a bit peckish and fancy some *tiffin* as you bloody former Colonial wasters call it.'

'That isn't for *you*!' Miss Frithington-Babcock yelped as the television critic started to raise the white confection towards his mouth. 'And you *mustn't* – um – eat it!'

'*Mustn't* my arse-hole!' Tremayne spat out coarsely and took a big bite.

'I did try to – um – *stop* him, Amelia,' the Deputy Headmistress stated, watching the television critic munching away and spitting out crumbs in his eagerness to stuff more of the tasty confection into his mouth. 'He wouldn't – um – *listen* to me.'

'No, Hortense,' Miss Benkinsop replied. 'He *wouldn't.* Well, on *his* head be it!'

Watched by the teachers, who he was convinced he had so quelled by his menacing attitude they did not dare offer any resistance, Tremayne finished the cake without wondering about the Headmistress's cryptic remark. Deliberately spilling some on to the polished top of the desk, causing Miss Frithington-Babcock to dart a warning glance which halted the retaliatory action she realized her superior was on the point of launching, he helped himself to a cup of tea and drank it with a slurping sound they found as irritating and disgusting as it was intended to be.

'All right,' the television critic said, after giving a belch and dropping the cup on to the thick carpet, which prevented it from being broken. Wishing he could 'pass wind' loudly to emphasise his willingness to lower himself to the level of the 'little people' he pretended to respect, admire and represent politically, he continued, 'I'm off now.'

'Let me say I don't expect to see you again,' Miss Benkinsop answered, clenching her hands as an aid to keeping her temper under control. 'Goodbye.'

Grinning and thinking of the extra set of negatives in his jacket's breast pocket, behind the envelope holding what he regarded as no more than the first deposit for the blackmail, Tremayne walked across the large entrance hall. He was just about to go through the open front double doors when, to the accompaniment of giggles and shouts, several girls came in. Clad alike in white training 'sneakers', matching ankle socks, flaring black micro-skirts and open necked, short sleeved navy blue blouses – with a décolleté, a sufficiently thin material and snug fit indicating each wearer was well endowed physically – all were in their late 'teens. The speed at which they made their entrance caused him to be surrounded and crushed amongst them in a way which any normal man would have found most enjoyable, but he regarded as distasteful. However, he was not in such close proximity for many seconds.

After the girls had passed on, continuing to behave as he expected of pampered pupils at an expensive public school, the television critic slouched across the parking area and boarded his car. Having started the vehicle moving, he remembered what kind of parents sent their girls to Benkinsop's Academy For The Daughters Of Gentlefolk. A sensation of alarm bit into him and he instinctively clutched at the jacket over the breast pocket. With a sensation of relief, he felt the expected bulge there and decided he had nothing to fear.

'What the hell else did I expect?' Tremayne told himself. 'The parents might all be villains, but their daughters won't be getting taught to pick pockets at a posh place like this!'

Filled with smug self satisfaction at a lucrative piece of blackmail having been concluded satisfactorily, the television critic decided to try some of his other victims before letting Miss Benkinsop know he had more photographs and negatives for her to purchase. He was so filled with thoughts of the rosy future he felt sure lay ahead, he did not notice an attractive and stylishly dressed woman in her late twenties who had boarded a red sports car at the other end of the parking area and was following him. After having covered some ten miles of the return journey to London, still without being aware of his pursuer, a feeling of lassitude came over him and, drawing into the lay-by he was approaching, he stopped the vehicle. By the time the woman was passing, his hands had flopped from the steering wheel and his head was tilted back as if he had fallen asleep.

* * *

Charles Tremayne would have learned he was in error about the curriculum of the School if he had seen Amanda Tweedle break away from the rest of the Sixth Formers and go to Miss Benkinsop's study!

'Here they are, ma'am,' the School Swot said, placing the envelope holding the money and another which was flat on the desk. 'He did have some more negatives, as you expected, but I don't think he will find out they're gone if he just feels at his jacket and doesn't reach inside the pocket. I put in the substitute envelope and there is *no* way whatsoever it and its contents can be traced back here.' Then her gaze went to where Miss Frithington-Babcock was mopping up the spilled tea. 'Oh dear, he did make a *mess*.'

'Nothing that can't be cleaned away,' Miss Benkinsop replied. 'And he certainly enjoyed your Angel Cake, Hortense.'

'I've never given it to anybody who – um – *didn't*,' the Deputy Headmistress replied, but managed to sound modest, thinking of the numerous people who had sampled her wares over the years. 'That *dreadful* British Communist Party woman working like so many more of them with the Nazi spy-ring we dealt with in '39 even asked me for the recipe, but I wasn't in time to give it to her, even if I had been so inclined the way she was betraying her country. Not that she could have made it exactly the same anyway. She wouldn't have the special mushrooms from the depths of the Amazon jungle for the flavouring. I, of course, grow my own.'

Returning the money to the safe behind the portrait of the Miss Amelia Penelope Diana Benkinsop whose ability as a dancer had brought ownership of the mansion, the present incumbent was satisfied with the way her plan had worked. Her judgement of character had suggested correctly how Tremayne would react to the sight of Miss Frithington-Babcock and the confection on the tray in particular. However, as a precaution, the tea had also been treated with powder from the extremely lethal poisonous type of mushrooms which were employed to produce the special qualities of the Deputy Headmistress's Angel cake. Having thought of a way in which to avoid the chance of the exchange being prematurely detected, she had persuaded Tremayne to put the money into a distinctive envelope and had had a duplicate containing pieces of blank paper made. Despite his sexual proclivities having rendered the distraction by the other Sixth Formers less effective than it would have proved with a normal man, switching the envelopes undetected had been child's play to Amanda and, as they would be told later by the young woman at that moment following the television critic, the ploy had produced the desired result.

'Fan-Dancer to base!' Miss Bettina 'Peaches' Pedlar called over the two-way radio which the School Swot had fitted into her sports car and adjusted to a wavelength and strength unlikely to be received by any chance listener in the British Isles, some fifteen minutes after having followed Tremayne from the School. She was using as her call-sign the type of performance she had specialized in before accepting the post as teacher for the Folk Dancing class. 'He's gone off right where F-B said he would.'

'Good,' Miss Benkinsop replied into the microphone of the receiving set placed on her desk by the School Swot. She felt relief at hearing the television critic's vehicle was brought to a stop without putting the lives of the other people on the road in danger. 'Thank you, Fan Dancer.'

Replacing the handset of the radio, the Headmistress gave a contented sigh. The would-be blackmailer had been dealt with and was now unable to make another attempt. What was more, the inevitable autopsy would be unable to establish anything except he had apparently died of natural – if undiscoverable – conditions. There was no longer any danger of the 'Screws Of Lower Grebe A.S.G.' having their participation exposed to the newspapers and they would be able to compete in the return Tag Team Debate against 'Benkers' Blonde Bombshells' without even learning the threat existed. What was more, the precautions which Amanda had already put into operation would ensure nothing else of the kind happened during a Debating Evening at Benkinsop's Academy For The Daughters Of Gentlefolk.

PART THREE

RITA YARBOROUGH, COMPANY 'Z', TEXAS RANGERS *In* THE DEADLY DREAMS

'God damn it, Alicia!' boomed an irate masculine voice with the accent of a Texan – which was not surprising considering the location – who had had a good education. 'Do you mean to stand there and tell me that you didn't bet the two hundred dollars I gave you on Dollrags like I said?'

'Please don't be *cross* with me, Ranse-honey,' pleaded a feminine speaker, whose origins were just as clearly from a similar stratum of society somewhere in New England. 'After seeing that poor man knocked down by a truck on the way here, I just *had* to make a bet on a horse called *Black And Blue*. I was sure it was a *sign*—!'

'Some *sign*!' the first voice barked just as irascibly, annoyance preventing the man from caring that his words were carrying to everybody in the immediate vicinity. 'The only god-damned *sign* I see is the one saying Dollrags *won* like I was *told* it would and that son-of-a-bitching badge-horse, Black And Blue, doesn't even *show*!'[1]

The time was shortly before one o'clock. It was a typically hot Monday afternoon early in June and the result of the horse race which had just ended was being announced on the large 'winners' board' and over the public address system at the recently opened track on the outskirts of Dallas, Texas. Standing face to face in the 'ring', apparently oblivious of everyone except themselves, the two speak-

1. 'Badge-horse': one of inferior ability, but which was taken from track to track so its owner would receive an 'owner's badge' to be used for the purposes of touting.

ers were such exceptionally fine examples of the Caucasian sub-species of *Homo Sapiens* they would be noticeable in any company.

Not long past her twenty-fifth birthday, 'Alicia' was five foot six in height and pretty without being excessively beautiful. Cut in a shortish, tousled, curly 'wind blown bob', her reddish-brown hair was all but concealed beneath the felt cloche hat with a velvet band which enveloped her head to the neck at the back and came to her eyes at the front. Although the current fashion called for a slim and boyish figure, even if attaining it required the strict adherence to a diet and the use of such a device as a Poiret-designed 'flattening brassiere', her shapely body only just fell short of the Junoesque 'hourglass' contours which had been all the rage a few decades earlier. The swell of her full and firm bosom, her trim waist and well rounded hips were exhibited all too clearly by the lime-green satin dress – cut daringly low at front and rear and leaving her arms bare – she wore. Adorned by a fringe of slightly longer tassels of the same material, its skirt ended just above knee level to display shapely legs in black 'fishnet' stockings, the calf muscles being set off in bold relief by her high heeled lime-green pumps. Long pendant earrings, several bracelets on each wrist and the lumpy rings gracing her fingers had the sparkle of diamonds. A further suggestion of wealth was the dainty gold lamé vanity bag she was clasping in her hands as she looked in conern at her companion.

Even in a crowd of Texans, who tended to be tall, 'Ranse-honey' stood out as a remarkably well developed physical specimen. About the same age as the girl, at first sight, everything about him exuded a similar indication of wealth. he towered over her by a good nine inches. Tilted back on his curly golden blond hair, a white J.B. Stetson hat with a low crown, a wide brim and a black leather band decorated by silver *conchas*, made him appear even taller. Almost classically handsome, his tanned face had an angry expression. His tremendously wide shoulders trimmed down to a slim, flat-bellied waist to produce a torso which was shown to its best advantage by the excellent fit of an obviously expensive and bespoke light-weight, single breasted light grey suede jacket of western cut. The rest of his attire gave indications of being equally costly. Open at the neck, his tan shirt was silk and embellished by a brightly multi-coloured cravat of the same material. His dark brown trousers, from the cuffs of which emerged the sharp toes of what could only be a pair of black Luskey's Hornback Lizard Western pattern boots, had just as clearly been made to his measure.

However, although some glances were directed their way, the exchange of remarks between the couple attracted little other attention from any but two of the people around them in the circle of bookmakers' stands where the majority of the betting on the race had been carried out. Despite the hostile tone of the man, nobody offered to intervene in a private argument. His physical appearance and obvious annoyance were deterrents in most cases. Furthermore, dedicated 'horse-players' being what they were – and still are – its subject was considered a matter of purely personal importance and his complaint, particularly in the opinion of the other male race-goers, was fully justified. Even the two people who were taking a more noticeable interest merely stood watching and listening.

'But the *sign*—!' 'Alicia' began.

'To hell with you and your god-damned *signs*,' 'Ranse-honey' growled, scowling even more unpleasantly. 'You cost me two hundred bucks and I won't have time to get it back, seeing I've got to go into town and report for du—*start work* right now.'

'Y—You'll come with me to the Banyan Club tonight, won't you?' the girl asked worriedly, as the blond giant started to turn away.

'I'll *think* on it,' 'Ranse-honey' snapped over his shoulder and, before striding away with a gait redolent of anger, went on, 'And don't you go calling me at the office to ask. I'll let you know the "yes" or "no" of it when *I'm* ready!'

'What a bad tempered young man,' commented a mellow voice with a Mid-West accent, after the blond giant had gone beyond hearing distance.

Turning, the girl found the speaker was a middle-aged man of about her height and with a build which could best be described as portly. Holding a white Panama hat in his right hand, he had thinning brown hair plastered back over his head in a not too successful attempt to cover its bald patches. Reddened more by good living than the sun, his sweat-soaked features were pleasantly bland and showed concern. He had on a moderately expensive brown pinstripe three-piece suit, a white shirt with an attachable celluloid collar and the kind of soberly striped tie often indicating membership of some social club or society. All in all, he gave the impression of being a fairly well-to-do, completely law-abiding and respectable member of the community; the kind who would always be willing to play the good Samaritan should, as at that moment, he consider the need had arisen.

Standing at the right side of the speaker, looking equally sympathetic, was a woman who could only be his wife. Perhaps three inches shorter, she too had a build which could be most generously classified as 'pleasing plump' and did nothing to flatter the tight bosomed and flare skirted white organdie summer dress she was wearing. It and the jewellery she had on enhanced the air of prosperity he exuded. Beneath a wide brimmed white straw hat, its crown innundated by small artificial flowers, was a mass of ringlets whose blonde colour was probably maintained by judicious employment of peroxide. She had a face which was amiable and not unattractive, albeit just a trifle over made-up in an unsuccessful attempt to give her a more youthful appearance. While nobody would take her for being much over forty, she would probably have been disappointed to know that neither would they have assumed she was any less. In her left hand, she clutched a bulky black handbag which did not go with the rest of her ensemble and she twirled a parasol in what she imagined to be a graceful fashion with her right hand.

'Such *bad* manners,' the woman supported in a high-pitched and somewhat squeaky voice most compliment-ary to her appearance and indicative of similar origins to her companion. Everything about her suggested she would always be willing to offer a helping hand, but was likely to be more well meaning than intelligent in her employment of it. 'I don't know what young men are coming to. They were so much more polite and *understanding* in my day. Are you all right, my dear?'

'Y—Yes,' 'Alicia' sniffed, glancing past the couple as if in search of somebody. Not, however, in the direction taken by the blond giant. An expression which might have been annoyance came over her attractive face, as if she was disappointed in something. However, it quicky passed and she returned her gaze to the woman and went on, 'It's all right, thank you.'

'I trust you don't think it impertinent of us to address you like this, my dear young lady?' the man inquired, his manner pompous and pedantic, yet continuing to suggest sympathy for one who he considered had been treated badly. 'Without being formally introduced and appearing to be intruding on your purely personal affairs like this, I mean.'

'No, I don't think any such thing,' the girl replied. 'I suppose we were talking rather loudly and, anyway, I have to admit it was *my* fault, not betting on Dollrags as Ranse told me. But the *sign*—.'

'Ah yes, the *sign*!' the man said and he darted a signific-ant glance at the woman who nodded in conspiratorial concurrence. 'Again I trust you don't think it was with a deliberate attempt to eavesdrop, but we could not help overhearing what you and your—er—gentleman friend—were saying and we found your reason for selecting Black And Blue most *interesting*.'

'*Most*,' the woman supported emphatically. 'Why, Jervis, it is practically a *sign* in itself.'

'So it is, my dear, so it *is*!' the man agreed, nodding his head vigorously. 'Forgive us, my dear young lady. You must wonder what we're talking about?'

'Do you believe in *signs*?' 'Alicia' asked, showing interest.

'We certainly *do*,' the man confirmed. 'Perhaps you would care to come and lunch with us in the Pavilion Bar so we can discuss the matter further?'

'I would be delighted to do so,' the girl accepted, after another glance in the direction she had looked earlier. 'By the way, my name is Alicia Vanderburgh.'

'Delighted to make your acquaintance, my dear Miss Vanderburgh,' the man declared, holding out his pudgy right hand to be shaken. 'I am Jervis V. Woods and this is my good lady wife, Vanessa-Diedre.'

'It is so pleasant to get to know a kindred spirit,' the woman enthused, also shaking hands in a similarly limp fashion. 'Do you attend many seances?'

'Not as many as I would like,' the girl replied. 'But I'm very interested in all kinds of psychic phenomena.'

'So are we, my dear young lady,' the man asserted. 'So are we.'

'Why, isn't this a *coincidence*?' Vanessa-Diedre declared, trying to sound like an excited and frivolous young belle, although she looked somewhat too old for the pose to be successful. 'We've more in common than we realized, Jervis. Perhaps—!'

'Perhaps, my dear, *perhaps*,' Woods answered, looking in a mildly prohibitive fashion at his wife. 'But let us wait until we're having lunch before we go into *that*.'

* * *

'Actually, my dear Miss Vanderburgh—!' Jervis V. Woods said, exuding amiability combined with a touch of self-importance, after he, his wife and their guest were seated at a table clear of the few other diners in the race course's expensive Pavilion Bar. 'Or may we call you "Alicia"?'

'Of course you may,' the attractive and shapely girl assented.

'Well, *Alicia*,' the portly man continued, the emphasis he placed upon the name implying that a bond of friendship had been established. 'My dear lady wife and I are more than just merely *interested* in all kinds of psychic phenomena. In fact, Vanessa-Diedre is possessed of what I am *sure* must be unique psychic powers.'

'*Really*?' the girl asked, looking impressed. 'What form do they take?'

'I know it sounds hard to *believe*,' Woods declared. He paused for a couple of seconds before continuing dramatically. 'She can dream the *winners* of horse races.'

'Good heavens!' Alicia gasped, staring in what appeared to be awe at the plump blonde woman who beamed back at her in a delighted fashion. 'How very *useful* that must be for you.'

'It *would* be, although we have no *need* for the money we could win,' Woods replied. 'But there is a *problem*.'

'What is that?'

'As you can imagine, the psychic vibrations can only reach out once the race is in progress. However, the message has come and the inevitably correct outcome is *always* known to Vanessa-Diedre *before* it is over and the result announced.'

'Then I don't see the problem. Surely you could be waiting near a bookmaker and place your bet when the message comes?'

'Ah,' Woods sighed, shaking his head sadly. 'If it was only that *simple*.'

'You see, my dear,' the plump blonde went on. 'When the vibrations commence, I go into a trance and don't come out of it until after I've given the name of the horse which has come to me. But I must have darkness and *silence* to remain en-transified, if that is the word for it. We have found out by our experiments this morning that, even on the parking lot outside the track and sitting in our Packard with all the shades drawn, there was too much noise and the message couldn't get through.'

'Oh dear, how *unfortunate* for you,' the girl commiserated. 'And it is such a *pity* that your psychic gift must go to waste.'

'That it is,' Woods sighed. 'That it is!'

'If only there was *somewhere* in town we could get the be—*wagers* put on as soon during the race as the message comes,' Vanessa-Diedre supplemented, even more dismally. 'Just for *small* amounts, of course, and only in the interests of a *scientific* study of my powers.'

'I know one place where you can put them on,' Alicia declared. 'And for any amount you wish, right up to the result coming through in fact as they are in communication with the track on a private telephone line.' She gave a gasp and, having bitten her lip, said, 'Oh dear! I shouldn't have mentioned *that*. It is a secret only members are supposed to know.'

'You can count upon our silence, we would of course respect your confidence,' Woods reassured. 'But where might it be situated?'

'The Banyan Club,' the girl supplied, despite her comment about the need for secrecy where the private telephone line was concerned.

'The Banyan Club,' Woods repeated, looking interested.

'Well of all the coinci—!' the blonde began, her expressive face showing a similar emotion.

'It is, my dear,' Woods interrupted, then he gave a cluck of annoyance. 'But that doesn't *help* us. We aren't members and I've been told the Banyan Club has such a long waiting list for membership, its committee won't accept anybody like us who are only making a short stay in Dallas.'

'I've been a member ever since I arrived in town, Daddy saw to *that*,' Alicia stated with pride, the establishment in question being currently the most exclusive and expensive in Dallas. 'So I could take you there and introduce you as my guests.'

'Why that would be *splendid*!' Vanessa-Diedre enthused, clapping her hands and bouncing a couple of times on her chair in a girlish fashion not entirely becoming one of her less than slender build.

'It would, my dear, and we are both *most* grateful for the offer,' Woods went on, but his manner showed he had reservations and he explained them. 'However, even if you could find the privacy to become en-transified on the premises and there was the *absolute* quiet you need for your revelation to break through the astral plane, there might not be sufficient time when it reaches you for us to get the wager placed before the result arrives at the Club.'

'I would *never* have thought of that, dear,' the blonde claimed, slapping her palms together and beaming in admiration at her husband. Then swinging her gaze to the girl, she continued in a similarly impressed tone, 'Do you see just how fortunate I am to have such an intelligent spouse, Alicia-dear?'

'Such praise will be making me *blush*, my dove,' Woods warned, in an amiable and gently chiding manner before becoming more solemn. 'And, anyway, my being so "intelligent", as you put it, has only shown me why it won't be any *use* for us to avail ourselves of Alicia's kind offer.'

'There *must* be *some* way of doing it,' the girl stated, with a pouting vehemence which suggested she had more than an altruistic reason for wanting to be of assistance.

'Good heavens!' Vanessa-Diedre yelped excitedly. 'There *is* a way. That is what I meant by a coincidence when you mentioned the Banyan Club in the bookmakers' ring, dear. The house we're renting is alongside the Club and I'm *sure*, not that I'm the prying and nosy kind, that we can see into some of its windows.'

'*Which* side?' Alicia inquired, showing excitement again.

'The west, I think it would be,' the blonde supplied.

'It is, my dear,' Woods confirmed.

'You are so right about it being a *coincidence*!' the girl breathed, seeming to be close to overawed by the turn of events. 'In fact it is a *sign* in itself. The gaming-room is on the left side.'

'Then there just *might* be a way in which we can utilize your *gift*, my dove!' the portly man declared. 'If Alicia is willing to help us, that is.'

'I'll do *anything* I can,' the girl promised eagerly. 'In the interests of psychic research, of course.'

'Of course,' Woods replied. 'But you could also have a few *small* wagers of your own, if you don't mind doing so when you know you are *certain* to *win*.'

'You could win back your gentleman friend's two hundred dollars,' Vanessa-Diedre suggested. 'And enough more to impress him with your astute reading of the *signs*.'

'Good heavens, so I *could*!' Alicia answered, trying to give the impression that she had not already been thinking along those lines.

'But you must promise us not tell him, or *anybody* else how you obtain the winners,' Woods warned. 'If you do, not only might it be thought *illegal* by the men with whom you place the wagers—!' He paused, then continued in a reassuring fashion when the girl flashed a hand to her mouth and showed alarm at the prospect, 'Although I don't for the life of me see how it could *possibly* be. However, Vanessa-Diedre and I wish to avoid any of the publicity which would arise if the news of what we can achieve got out before we have presented our findings to the Psychic Phenomenon Research Centre.'

'I can understand why you *would*,' Alicia admitted, but her attitude made it apparent that the consideration was far from being uppermost in her mind. 'When can we start to win—the *experiment*?'

'Why not as soon as we have had our lunch?' the blonde suggested. 'If that is all right with *you*, Alicia?'

'It certainly *is*!' the girl affirmed eagerly. Then her head gave a jerk redolent of annoyance. 'Damn it! I've an appointment with Louis of Paris for this afternoon, the hairdresser from France *everybody* is trying to go to you know. Oh well, I'll go and call to say I will have to postpone it, because some family business I can't put off has cropped up. That should satisfy them. This is too *good*—er, *important* to miss.'

'We've *got* her, Vannie,' Woods commented in a vastly different tone than he had employed up to that moment, watching Alicia hurry towards the telephone booths at the side of the room.

'That we have,' Vanessa-Diedre agreed, also sounding and looking harder and more decisive. 'Damn it, Jerv, I could hardly believe the luck when I heard her talking about her "signs" and taking that big feller to the Banyan Club.'

'She's fallen for *everything* we told her hook, line and sinker and will do what she's told,' the portly man declared, his hobby being fishing although he kept its terms out of his speech when working. 'Just so she doesn't call and spill it to that feller, as well as cancelling her hair-dresser's appointment. Unless I'm mistaken, there was a gun under the left side of his jacket.'

'I noticed that,' the blonde admitted. 'In fact, I'd say from the way he was dressed, he's a copper of some kind and one who's on the take. No honest badge would have enough cash to spare for making two hundred dollar bets, even if he expected to win.'

'Why'd he be chancing his own money when he's latched on to a rich girl friend, though?' Woods queried, watching the girl starting to make the call.

'He maybe needed more for something than she could hand over,' Vanessa-Diedre guessed. 'And he figured, or she'd said something which made him guess she'd put it on Black And Blue instead of Dollrags. So he was counting on getting the money off her when it lost, or he'd collect from the bookie if she did as he said and Dollrags won. Either way, *he* couldn't *lose*. She's so daffy about him that she'd be willing to make good the money she'd lost for him – and more, most likely – if he kept her dangling a while instead of agreeing to go with her to the Banyan Club straight off. She doesn't need to worry. Unless I've got him pegged all wrong, he knows he's on to too good a thing not to go with her.'

'You're right,' Woods asserted. 'Anyway, if it looks like she's going to make more than the one call, you go over and stop her.'

If the couple could have heard what was being said in the telephone booth, they would not have been so contented with the way they believed things were going for them!

'It's Rita, Jubal,' Alicia announced, implying she had

not spoken the truth when introducing herself to her host and hostess. What was more, the rest of her information did not concern cancelling an appointment with the city's most sought after ladies' hairdresser. '*He* didn't bite, but I think somebody else *has*.'

* * *

'Well, well, well!' breathed the attractive, rusty-brown haired young woman whose name was not 'Alicia Vanderburgh', looking in the back of the massive black 1924 Packard Super Eight in the garage. Although she had been given different instructions, she had taken the opportunity to enter and satisfy her suppositions when the chauffeur who brought it there went to the house without having locked the door. 'I thought that must be how they did it.'

It was just after half past eight in the evening and Rita Yarborough, which was her true identity, was continuing the self-appointed task she had commenced by chance at the race course that afternoon.

Far from being naive and love-struck, although she was wealthy, the girl had been playing a part in an operation being carried out by the elite and unpublicised Company 'Z' of the Texas Rangers, to which she had earned the right to be considered an official 'unofficial' member.[2] However, the apparently disagreeable discusssion between herself and Sergeant Ranse Smith had not been intended for the benefit of Jervis V. and Vanessa-Diedre Woods. Instead, they had been hoping to arouse the interest and cause a visiting gangster from the East to seek to make her acquaintance.[3] The ploy had failed to produce the desired results. Nevertheless, because they had struck her as being too good to be true, she had decided the couple who

2. *Information about Rita Yarborough's involvement with Company 'Z', Texas Rangers, is given in:* APPENDIX TWO.

3. *What the assignment entailed is told in:* Part Three, *Persona Non Grata,* MARK COUNTER'S KIN.

apparently offered commiserations were worth investigation. It was a tribute to her own histrionic ability that she had persuaded them to accept her in the role she had created for their benefit.

Having no doubt that some form of trickery was planned against the Banyan Club rather than her *alter ego*, and keeping watch to make sure neither the man or the woman came over to check upon who she was calling, Rita had reported her failure where the gangster was concerned and her suspicions with regards to Woods to the member of Company 'Z' in command of the operation. Admitting there was justification for the supposition, but pointing out that none of the Rangers would be available to give her support should it be needed, Sergeant Jubal Branch had been reluctant to accede to her request to follow the matter up. Promising she would be careful and reminding him of how she had managed to handle her most recent assignment, the first she had carried out independently instead of having the backing of one of the men,[4] she had been given his permission with the proviso that she kept him informed of developments and took no chances.

Rejoining the couple at the conclusion of the call, Rita had decided the time she had taken might have aroused their suspicion. She had explained it had needed much longer than she anticipated before she had finally managed to persuade Louis of Paris to merely postpone the hairdressing appointment until later in the week instead of cancelling it altogether. Having done so and feeling sure the story was accepted, she had taken a somewhat perverse delight in having a most enjoyable and costly lunch at their expense. Just before it was over, a burly man in a chauffeur's uniform had come into the Bar and, apologising politely, Woods had crossed to talk to him. Although no explanation for the conversation was given

4. Rita Yarborough's first independent assignment is recorded in: Part Two, 'Behind A Locked And Bolted Door', MORE J.T.'S LADIES.

when her host returned, on leaving the race track, she had discovered they were to travel to the city in a taxi.

While walking through the parking lot to the taxi rank, Woods had pointed out the Packard with what was intended to be taken for pride of possession, although the girl concluded he was more concerned with proving its existence as further 'evidence' of his financial stability. He had apologised for not being able to use it to take her to their destination, claiming neither he nor his wife could drive and their chauffeur, who was too valuable to risk losing, had stated a disinclination to leave before the results of the last race had allowed him to ascertain whether he had any winnings forthcoming. Saying her father had similar problems, Rita made no reference to an item she noticed on the vehicle which she knew was far from being a usual accessory on such a car. In fact, because of the size of the set and its batteries, having a wireless installed in even so big a motor car was generally considered impractical.

Ordering the taxi to stop a couple of blocks from their destination, Woods had used his and his wife's 'less than slender' condition as an excuse for them to get out and 'stretch their lower limbs' by walking the rest of the way. Despite realizing this was intended to avoid letting the driver see where they were going, Rita had raised no objections. The property to which she was guided was everything she expected in such a 'high-rent' area. Standing in its own grounds, which were maintained in such excellent condition the lawns showed signs of having been mowed that morning, the house was large and in a similar 'colonial' style to its neighbours on each side. However, while approaching along the wide gravel path, the portly man apologised in advance for there not being any servants on the premises and explained he had given them all the day off as he and his wife had expected to spend all of it at the races.

Looking around on entering, the girl had had to admit the pair were thorough. They had in all probability rented the property from whichever domestic servant had been left in charge while the owners were absent, but she could see nothing to prove this was the case. Whatever the condition of the rooms beyond the closed doors at ground level might be, the entrance hall and the one into which she was escorted on the second floor gave the impression of being in constant use.

Judging by appearances, Rita decided she had been brought into what was used as an upstairs' sitting-room. It had the necessary furniture for such a purpose and, besides the door through which she had entered, there were two more giving access, she guessed, into the adjoining rooms. Taking her to the window, Woods had drawn the drapes a little way apart. Looking across the garden, which was only some twenty yards in width at that side of the building, she could see the second floor of the Banyan Club and, more significantly, the window of the gaming-room, at about the same distance beyond the wall between the properties.

It soon became obvious that the couple had given considerable thought to putting their scheme into effect since coming to Dallas, or – more likely in the girl's estimation – had used it enough times elsewhere to have the system well worked out. Producing some large cards, which bore numbers from one to twenty in big red letters, the portly man had told her what was expected from the part 'Alicia Vanderburgh' was to play. While his wife was lying on the bed in the darkened room on the right, undergoing the 'trances' which produced the 'revelations', she was to wait near the window of the Club's gaming-room. She was to have a copy of the *Dallas Sentinel* open at the racing page and keep watch on the casement where they were standing. As soon as the 'message' came, he would display the number of the winning horse on the list for the race and she would put down the wager immediately. Pointing out the 'spiritual guidance' only arrived shortly before the result was achieved and that there would be no time to lose if she was to beat the telephone call from the track giving the outcome, he had emphasised the need for haste.

Agreeing to do as she was asked, Rita had not been surprised when Woods suggested he bet a larger sum than had been intimated when the proposal was put to her. He had explained the increase in stakes by saying it seemed unfair not to capitalize upon his wife's 'heaven-sent gift', as the money which was won could be donated to the furtherance of research into psychic phenomenon and, having guessed this would be the case, the girl had raised no objections. Clearly wishing to avoid granting her *alter ego* an opportunity to change her mind, or have misgivings, the couple had given her five hundred dollars and sent her to wait for the signal which would notify her of how to wager on the next race. Still acting as a gracious host, the man had accompanied her to the front door and she was not presented with a chance to see into the room in which the 'revelations' would take place and verify her suspicions. However, having heard him lock the door as she walked away, she had seen enough when looking at the mansion while approaching the Club to satisfy her that her deductions were correct.

Although Sergeant Jubal Branch and the manager were waiting in the entrance hall when Rita arrived, there had not been sufficient time for her to talk with them immediately. Instead, promising to go into details later, she had entered the gaming-room and, as instructed, allowed herself to be seen by Woods at the window. He had also held up a board as he promised and she gave the pre-arranged signal indicating she was able to read the number on it.

About fifteen minutes later, the man was back at the window and showing a board marked '7'. Checking the newspaper, Rita discovered this was a horse called 'Leading Light' and at odds of three to one. She had time to place the five hundred dollars on it to win before a red light, signifying the result was coming in, was flashed over the closed door of the room with the telephone line to the track. Having returned to the window and given the sign arranged to notify Woods of the successful transaction, she was free to move away and explain what was happening to the two men waiting in the entrance hall.

The manager had been furious and wanted to go straight to the mansion and have the couple arrested. However, the lean and leathery old sergeant had agreed with the girl that such precipitate action would be unwise. As yet, although the men had agreed with her theory of how it was carried out, there was no evidence to prove a swindle was being worked. What was more, as the link between the conspirators could be broken so easily – and would be at the first hint of trouble – the proof would not be forthcoming. Being so experienced, they would keep all the downstairs entrances and the doors of the upstairs' rooms fastened. Therefore, by the time access could be made by force, they would have taken the necessary precautions to ensure the worst which could happen would be to prevent them from repeating the trick against the Banyan Club. Being wealthy in her own right, Rita had promised to make good any losses which might be incurred by the delay and Branch had declared his superior would also ensure the Club would not be the loser. This had prompted the manager, who was also one of the owners, to assert neither would be necessary and he would do as they requested.

There had only been three more races and the results proved the system was not infallible. Although Joyous Event upheld its name by producing a win, albeit at 'odds on' of four to one,[5] no number had been displayed for the preceeding race and the one which followed – the last of the day – saw a complaint against the winner for some infraction of the rules lodged and upheld after Rita was informed of its name and had placed her bet. Nevertheless, there had still been a good sum of money from the two fortunate wagers and, on receiving it, Woods had expressed complete satisfaction. When 'Alicia Vanderburgh' complained about having lost all her previous winnings on the last race, he pointed out that such things had to be expected and he had advised her not to increase the

5. For the benefit of those readers who are not familiar with the terminology of wagering, 'odds on' means the horse in question is so well fancied to win the race that the better must, in this instance, stake four units to win one.

stakes. However, he had also given her 'comfort' by reminding her 'tomorrow is another day' and, particularly as the losses would serve to reduce the chance of suspicion, they would continue to employ the system if she was in agreement. Declaring she was, Rita had parted company with the couple before their car returned from the race track.

Doing as she had said she would, when Woods apologised for not being able to supply transport to the hotel at which she was staying, Rita returned to the Club and took one of the taxis which were waiting on the rank. She had been joined when out of sight of the mansion by Branch – who had set off on foot when she emerged – and his big bluetick coonhound. During the journey, they held a council of war. It had been agreed a 'stakeout' must be mounted on the couple, to ensure they did not decide to call their ploy quits and leave Dallas with the money already gathered.

However, because of the delicate nature of the operation upon which Company 'Z' was engaged in the city, the girl and the elderly sergeant could not call upon the services of the local peace officers and would have to attend to the matter with their own resources. This had raised a problem. Apart from them, there was only Sergeant Ranse Smith in the vicinity and he would not be available because of their main assignment. What was more, Branch had to help him with the next stage of their plan that evening. Therefore, once again being warned not to take any chances, Rita was assigned the duty of keeping watch on the mansion. If the suspects left, she was to follow and take the first opportunity of notifying Branch of the direction in which they were travelling.

Going to her room at the hotel, the girl had taken off her 'flapper's' style of clothing and, with relief as she did not care for such ostentatious adornment, the jewellery which was used to help her pose as a wealthy, less than intelligent, socialite. Then she had taken a shower to remove the excessive amount of makeup she found equally distasteful. Feeling clean and refreshed, she had donned a masculine peaked cap, an open necked dark blue blouse with a much less revealing décolleté than that of the dress, the 'bell-bottomed' trousers from a pair of royal blue beach pyjamas, a lightweight brown leather windcheater and Western style riding boots. To complete the ensemble, she had placed a Remington Double Derringer two shot pistol in a small black handbag. She then took another precaution for her self protection. Then, collecting her Buick Sport Tourer from the garage, she raised its top to give concealment and drove to the mansion.

As she slowly passed the front gates, Rita saw that the main entrance to the garage was open and the Packard was not inside. She wondered whether the couple had decided to take no further chances and had left. What disturbed her most was realizing she could not do anything except inform Branch if this should be the case and there was no way she could contact him for at least two more hours. Accepting the situation, she elected to wait until after dark, then go to check whether they had taken their departure. Parking in a position which would give the impression that the Buick had been left there while its owner was visiting the Banyan Club, or a house across the street, she settled down to mount her surveillance.

Much to her relief, just as the girl was about to commence the reconnaisance, the big car passed her vehicle and turned into the drive. Although the thing which attracted her attention when leaving the race track was no longer to be seen, the black curtains were still drawn over all the rear windows and the front seat was unoccupied except for the chauffeur. Having seen it approaching, she had ducked down and she felt sure he would think the Buick had been left unattended. Nor had anything occurred to make her change her mind. The chauffeur turned along the drive to the garage after having taken the car in, and lowered the front entrance from the inside.

Noticing the chauffeur did not lock the door through which he emerged, Rita concluded she was being offered an opportunity to check up on her suppositions. Waiting until he had gone into the house, putting aside the nagging memory of the instructions for her behaviour given by Branch, she picked up the handbag and left her vehicle. Slipping cautiously through the still open front gates, she made a circuitous way across the lawn until arriving at her destination.

Opening the left side passenger door of the Packard and producing a small electric torch from her handbag, the girl directed its beam at the interior. As she had expected, the back seat was occupied by the kind of transportable wireless transmitting set – with a Morse code key, batteries to supply power, and the aerial which she had first seen in the operating position at the race track's parking lot and which had supplied her first clue to what was happening – which the military and law enforcement agencies were beginning to use in increasing numbers.

Just as Rita was making the *sotto voce* comment of self congratulation, the side door of the garage was jerked open!

'There, what'd I tell you?' snarled a voice with a Brooklyn accent, as a switch clicked and the interior was flooded with light. 'There *was* somebody casing the joint in that Buick!'

* * *

'You told us, East-Side!' Jervis V. Woods admitted dryly, coming into the garage with a Smith & Wesson Army Model of a 1917 revolver in his right hand. He was speaking over his shoulder to where his wife and the chauffeur, the latter armed in the same way, followed close behind him. As they moved forward until standing on either side of him, he looked closer at the intruder and continued, 'It seems our pigeon was smarter than we imagined, my dear.'

'That's how it looks,' Vanessa-Diedre Woods agreed, gesturing with the four inch barrel of the Colt Police Positive revolver in her right hand. She no longer employed her earlier behaviour or speech and, while its calibre was only .32 Long as opposed to the .45 of the other two handguns, she looked as capable of using the weapon effectively as was her husband. 'So toss that bag over here straight away, girlie!'

'Had any more *dreams*?' Rita Yarborough inquired, restraining her right hand before it could enter the handbag, and doing as she was ordered.

'You'll find they're pretty deadly dreams for you,' the woman claimed, deftly catching the bag in her left hand and scowling at the girl in a menacing fashion. 'Because you know too much about us to be let stay alive.'

'That sounds *threatening*,' Rita commented quietly.

'You'll soon enough find it's more than just *sounds* threatening,' Vanessa-Diedre warned. having made the pronouncement, she thumbed the top of the bag open. After glancing inside, she held it so her husband could do the same. 'Look, Jerv', she's got a stingy-gun in here!'

'It might only be a novelty cigarette lighter,' Rita suggested, standing with her hands dangling by her sides in an attitude suggestive of being completely at ease.

'And you *might* be the feather-brained flapper you had us figuring you for,' Vanessa-Diedre countered, tipping the contents of the bag on to the floor and stirring them with her left toe. 'She might be packing a rod, but she doesn't have a badge or anything else to show who she is.'

'So I see, my dear,' Woods replied, but there was a hardness underlying the way he said the words, even though they were in his usual tone.

'What are you, girlie,' the blonde challenged. 'A female cop, or a Pink-Eye gumshoe in skirts?'

'These are beach pyjama trousers and I'm not *either*,' Rita answered truthfully. She was recognized as a peace officer only by the other members of Company 'Z' and the very few highly placed dignitaries in the State Legislature who were aware of its existence, and she had no connection with the Pinkerton National Detective Agency. Then, having sought to convince her captors that she was not afraid of them by her correction to the description of her attire, she continued with her attempt to lessen the danger. The means she selected did not imply an official capacity. However, she felt it would be even more effective with people who were obviously seasoned criminals and who would appreciate the ramifications behind her explanation. 'But, before you do something you'll wish you *hadn't*, I *am Rapido* Clint's girl friend.'

'*Rapido* Clint!' East-Side almost yelped and, although they had somewhat better control over their emotions, the girl could see the couple were as disturbed as she had hoped by what was, in fact, genuine information as far as it went.

'*Rapido* Clint,' Rita repeated, feeling pleased at the effect she had achieved by announcing an association with a young man known to the underworld as a very competent professional killer. However, while they were on close terms and would become even closer,[6] he was actually Sergeant Alvin Dustine Fog of Company 'Z'. 'In fact, that is who I was with at the race track.'

'But you called him—!' Vanessa-Diedre began, darting a glance of concern at her husband.

'Of course I called him "Ranse-honey",' the girl scoffed, placing her hands on her hips without arousing any protest from the trio. 'Even if we hadn't been trying to get close to a mark he has a contract on, with the chance of race track bulls and other cops being around, I'd hardly be saying, "*Rapido*-honey" as loudly as I was talking, now *would* I, *Jervis*?'

'She's lying in her teeth, boss!' East-Side suddenly growled, losing his air of perturbation, as the use of the other man's christian name caused the blonde to glare even more angrily at the girl. 'I done like you telled me when I come to see you in the Bar at the track and checked on the feller she was with. He ain't *Rapido* Clint. His name's Ranse Smith and he's a copper with the Dallas Police Department who's living way over his head 'n' up to his ears in debt.'

'Is that *so*?' Vanessa-Diedre spat out. 'It's a pity you're not

6. Rita Yarborough eventually married Alvin Dustine 'Cap' – as he was called by the time the ceremony took place, in tribute to being one of the youngest men ever to attain the rank of captain in the Texas Rangers – Fog and it is from them we obtained the documents upon which this narrative is based.

as god-damned smart as you think you are, you puffed-out chested *bitch*!'

'It's a pity *you* don't look less of a raddled *old* hag, you *bottle blonde*,' the girl replied, picking each word carefully in the belief they would provoke the kind of response she was seeking.

The selection proved correct!

There was nothing more calculated to arouse the worst of Vanessa-Diedre's quick and bad temper than any mention of her age!

Even before they had decided they had found a sucker to help them carry out their scheme to swindle the Banyan Club, the blonde had noticed her husband studying 'Alicia Vanderburgh's' far from hidden feminine attributes in a way with which she was no longer favoured. However, although annoyed, she had taken consolation from the thought that the girl was apparently proving as stupid as they hoped. What was more, in addition to making them a considerable sum of money, she would be the first to suffer the consequences should anything go wrong and, in fact, the only one provided their precautions proved as effective as in other places where they had operated.

The mocking words removed all of the smug satisfaction which had remained, bringing to a boil the vicious nature which lay close beneath the veneer of Vanessa-Diedre's working *persona*. Letting out a close to animalistic screech of fury, she darted forward and swung up the revolver with the intention of using its barrel to deliver a pistol-whipping which would leave the mocking and attractive face a bloody ruin. By doing so, she was behaving just as her intended victim hoped she would.

Always a tomboy and often involved in physical scuffles while growing up, Rita had had her ability at self protection developed still further by the instruction received since she became accepted as a member of Company 'Z'. This had included lessons from Alvin Fog in the very effective unarmed combat techniques he frequently employed to deal with larger and heavier antagonists.

Throwing up her arms, the girl crossed her wrists and interposed them so the descending arm entered the upper part of the 'X' they formed and halted long before the blow could be struck. Having stopped the attack, Rita retaliated with an equal efficiency. Sliding her right hand free, she clamped it upon the woman's wrist and just as swiftly brought the left to join it. Then, pivoting at the waist, she propelled her left knee into Vanessa-Diedre's stomach with all the power she could produce from legs strengthened by long hours of horseback riding. An explosive belching cry of pain burst from the woman and, letting the revolver fall from her fingers, she started to fold at the waist while being driven towards the men in an involuntary retreat.

Releasing her hold, Rita sprang backwards and sidestepped quickly behind the rear of the Packard. As she went, her right hand flashed down and behind her back to make the most of the second precautionary measure she had taken before leaving the hotel. Closing around the butt, she slid free one of the recently issued Colt Detective Special revolvers which she was carrying in a holster tucked under the waistband of the pyjama trousers. Not only did the two and a half inch long barrel allow for easy concealment, it greatly facilitated the speed of withdrawal. Pulling the weapon clear and bringing her left hand to join the other, although it had a double action which removed the need, she thumbed back its hammer as an aid to swifter discharge. Her every instinct warned this might be a very important factor.

Taken as unawares as Vanessa-Diedre had been over the way in which the girl responded to the attack, Woods was further impeded by his wife blundering in his direction and colliding with him. However, the chauffeur was to one side and showed signs of recovering his wits at a dangerous speed. Therefore, it was to him that Rita gave her attention first. Bringing the snub-nosed Colt to shoulder height and at arms' length, she started to take aim with the extra support offered by the double handed hold she had learned as another part of her education from the male members of Company 'Z'. Then her instincts and further training as a peace officer dictated her next actions.

'Drop it, mist—!' the girl began, conditioned to offer an opportunity to surrender even if doing so might put her own life in danger.

Instead of obeying, letting out a snarled profanity, East-Side thrust forward the Smith & Wesson. Realizing she had no other alternative, especially as the husband and wife were showing signs of separating, Rita sighted and fired in the only way she knew would offer her a chance of salvation under the circumstances. The weapon crashed before the chauffeur could complete his intention and the .38 Special bullet flew as directed. Struck between the eyes and killed instantaneously, he pitched backwards with the revolver flying from his lifeless grasp.

'Surrender!' Rita shouted, controlling the not inconsiderable recoil kick and again thumb-cocking the hammer as she turned the Detective Special's barrel towards the portly man and the blonde.

'Like hell!' Vanessa-Diedre hissed, twisting around and clear of her husband. Realizing the girl for whom she had developed such a hatred was once again threatening to get the better of them, her face became suffused by a rage which made her uncaring of the risks she was facing and she continued, 'You can't get *both* of us and the other one will get you!'

'Don't be *crazy*, damn it!' Woods snapped, looking into the muzzle of the revolver which was directed with disconcerting steadiness at the centre of his face. It was smaller in calibre than his own weapon, but did not strike him in such a light at that moment. Allowing the Smith & Wesson to drop from his hand, he continued, 'You saw how she took out East-Side and she can do it to *us*!'

'I'd listen to your man, was I you, ma'am,' drawled a masculine voice with a Texan's accent, coming from the doorway through which the trio had entered the garage. The words brought an end to the movement Vanessa-Diedre was starting to make in the direction of her husband's discarded weapon. ' 'Cause even in the *most* "on likely event-you-hillity's" Rita can't stop you, which I'm willing to bet's she could, ole Lightning 'n' me's more'n "caper-ribble" of helping out.'

Looking around, the portly man realized there was no hope whatsoever of carrying out his wife's desire for offensive action!

What was more, furious though she was, Vanessa-Diedre arrived at the identical conclusion!

Regardless of the mispronunciation, the newcomer posed a definite and unmistakable promise of support for the girl. Dressed after the fashion of a cowhand in town for a visit, which had changed little since the days of the open range system of raising cattle operated throughout much of the previous century, he was tall, lean and leathery of visage. His attire and the obviously well used ivory handled Colt Civilian Model Peacemaker in his gnarled right hand might be somewhat archaic to Eastern eyes,[7] but the latter was held with an air of relaxed competence indicative of considerable skill in its use. What was more, proving his official status, on the left lapel of his jacket was the silver 'star-in-a-circle' badge of a Texas Ranger.

Nor did the full potential menace of the peace officer's declaration end there. Standing by his side, looking as savage and unfriendly as a winter-starved timber wolf, was a big bluetick coonhound. Everything about it, from the bristling of hair along its back to the top lip drawn up to display a mouthful of large and sharp teeth, suggested it was only waiting for the least excuse to launch an attack.[8]

7. *Details of the different types of the Colt 'Single Action Army' Model P of 1873 revolver, more commonly known as 'the Peacemaker', are given in various volumes of the* Floating Outfit *series.*

8. *A detailed description of the bluetick coonhound, Lightning, is recorded in various volumes of the* Alvin Dustine 'Cap' Fog *series.*

'Hey, Jubal,' Rita greeted, showing relief although she did not let her Colt waver from its alignment. 'Nice of you to drop by.'

'Got done sooner'n I reckoned,' Sergeant Jubal Branch replied. 'Which being, I reckoned I'd best drift along over and relieve you for a spell. Found your car empty and "calker-rictated" 's how you'd likely come to do some "hin-vest-triggerating" 'spite of what I'd told you. So I allowed's I'd best sort of Injun over and see what was doing. Saw the light was on in here and concluded this'd be the place to look. Which it was.'

'You've *nothing* on us, officer!' Woods asserted, with what might have passed for righteous indignation. 'We saw somebody sneaking around and thought it was a burglar. So, exercising our rights as law-abiding citizens—!'

'Tell *that* to the judge,' Branch drawled. 'And I'll tell him's how I heard you threatening to make wolf bait out of this young lady.'

'It'll only be your word against ours,' Vanessa-Diedre pointed out sullenly.

'Which it would, was we to be 'resting you for that,' Branch replied. 'Only we're taking you in for trying to cheat the Banyan Club by having that jasper lying on the floor send you the winners from the race track in Morse code with a "wiry-less" set; which there's some's'd say that's the *least-wise* of your "pre-dical-mentations". You've heard tell of Hogan Turtle, I reckon?'

'Who might he b—!' Woods began, despite being aware the man in question was one of the leading figures in the law breaking circles of Texas.

'Just the man who bankrolls the Banyan Club, that's *all*,' Rita supplied and, knowing the blonde in particular would have been willing to have had her killed, derived satisfaction from the consternation which came to the faces of the couple as they realized the implications behind her information. 'And when he gets to hear what you tried, he'll probably decide to make an example of you to stop others getting similar ideas. But I wouldn't think about *that* if I was you, Vanessa-Diedre *darling*. It will give you some really deadly dreams.'[9]

9. What few qualms Rita Yarborough experienced over the extreme measures she was compelled to take in dealing with 'East-Side' ended when she was informed that he was wanted by the New York Police Department for having committed rape on three occasions and two brutal murders.

PART FOUR

CALAMITY JANE & BELLE STARR
In
DRAW POKER'S SUCH A *SIMPLE* GAME

Despite the large number of people on the sidewalks of a busy street in the business section of Topeka, or rather due to his desire to impress them, and two attractive female passengers with his skill, the young and newly appointed driver of the Wells Fargo stagecoach was keeping his six-horse team moving at a far greater speed than was wise for such a well populated area. However, it could not be said that he was entirely to blame for what happened next. Having watched him approaching with a fixed intensity, the well dressed young woman with a pretty face which was pale and distraught in its expression suddenly stepped into the street and started across it not too far ahead.

Letting out a startled exclamation, the driver responded to the danger with an admirable presence of mind. Applying the brake with his right boot, he let his whip slip between his legs. Then he braced both feet against the front of the driving box and, thrusting his body backwards, pulled with both hands on the reins in an attempt to either halt or turn the horses aside before they reached the young woman. Although the shotgun messenger at his side gave an unnecessary bellow of warning and grabbed for the leather ribbons to help, it was obvious even their combined efforts could not bring the powerful animals and fast moving vehicle to a stop in time to prevent an accident. In fact, it appeared nothing could save the young woman from her apparently imprudent and ill-advised actions.

Although masculine shouts and feminine screams arose from all sides, the person to respond most quickly to the situation was, despite her attire suggesting otherwise, most certainly *not* a man!

Five foot seven in height, in her late 'teens, the fastest to think and act had a battered dark blue U.S. Cavalry *kepi* perched at a rakish angle on her head. Her shortish and curly mop of fiery red hair framed a face which was tanned, freckled, pretty and generally merry looking. Rising firmly round and full, her breasts forced against the material of a well worn, but clean, fringed buckskin shirt which was open low enough at the neck to present a tantalising glimpse of the valley between the mounds. Trimming at the waist, obviously without any artificial aids, her torso expanded to form curvaceous hips fitting snugly into buckskin pants and set upon sturdily eye-catching legs. She had Pawnee moccasins on her feet and having the sleeves of the shirt rolled up above the elbows exposed arms more muscular than a lady of fashion would have cared for. Not that anybody would have suspected her of being one. Although her attire indicated she came from further west where such items were common, because of a ban imposed by the city's authorities, she did not have on a gunbelt and holstered revolver. However, the handle of a coiled, long-lashed bull whip was thrust through the leather loop attached at the left of the broad brown belt around her waist.

Hurtling from the raised sidewalk, the red head alighted running like a sprinter in a race over a much more level surface than the hard and wheel-rutted street. While she was achieving a most creditable speed, it would clearly be a very close thing whether she would achieve her purpose, or join the young woman as a victim of the rapidly approaching horses and stagecoach. Throwing herself through the air for the last few feet, after the fashion of a player performing a tackle in a 'Boston game',[1] she wrapped her arms around the slender waist of the woman. The

1. Based upon the variation of soccer first played at Rugby public school in England during 1823, the 'Boston game' would evolve into 'American' football.

impetus of her arrival carried them both onwards to safety, but with such a close margin that the wheels of the vehicle passed behind them by not more than a couple of inches.

Keeping going, unaware of just how narrow an escape they had had, the rescuer and the rescued were unable to retain their equilibrium and they sprawled to the ground at the feet of another person of their sex who had reacted with commendable promptitude, albeit an instant too late to be of assistance.

About an inch taller than the red head, of indeterminate age, the second would-be rescuer wore the black and white habit of a nun. Although such an item was not usual for her kind, she had on thin black leather gloves. Not unexpectedly, other than suggesting her figure might be more bulky than curvaceous, the conventional garments of her vocation prevented any indication of its contours from being revealed. Whatever good looks nature might have endowed upon her were marred by a pair of large, horn-rimmed spectacles and sallow features with a somewhat bulbous nose above prominent 'rabbit' teeth.

Although the nun had quit the opposite sidewalk with surprising speed for one of her appearance, she had come to a halt when she saw the girl would reach the young woman before she could. However, as they sprawled in a tangle together at her feet, she bent over them in a solicitous manner. Reaching out with both hands, she hooked them under the armpits of the buckskin shirt and lifted the red head erect.

If the ease with which the girl found herself elevated came as a surprise to her, what happened next was even more so!

'I'm real pleased you did that, Calam!' the nun whispered into the red head's ear, her accent being indicative of a well educated upbringing somewhere south of the 'Mason-Dixon' line. 'It would have drawn more attention my way than I need right now if I'd had to.'

* * *

'Thanks, sister,' the girl said, as she was released by the

woman in the habit of a nun, but whose words had indicated the attire was misleading.

Amongst her other talents, Martha 'Calamity Jane' Canary could justifiably consider herself an excellent poker player. In fact, she often claimed that nothing could surprise her. Nevertheless, she needed all the skill she had developed at controlling her emotions to avoid showing surprise over the words and the realization that the 'nun' was none other than the lady outlaw, Belle Starr.[2] Looking around quickly into the less than attractive face, she knew she would never have made the identification without receiving the evidence of the voice. Taking notice of what had been said, and drawing the required conclusion, even though she could not see any peace officers among the people who were gathering around, she refrained from saying anything which might inform them of the true state of affairs.

However, the response from the young woman who had been saved was hardly what might have been expected!

'Wh—Why did you have to *interfere*?' Ruby Wakefield asked in anguished tones which established her background was in the mid-West and of affluent circumstances.

'It seemed like a good thing to do,' Calamity answered coldly, puzzled by such an attitude on the part of a person she had rescued from serious injury, if not death, at some considerable risk to her own well being.

'I—I'm sorry,' the young woman replied with genuine contrition, looking from the red head to Belle Starr and back. 'But I didn't want sav—!'

'Don't say any more, my child,' the lady outlaw instructed, in a different tone to that used when addressing the red head. It had, in fact, lost its Southern drawl and taken on a timbre suggestive of Irish origins and with a note of authority such as a certain kind of nun

2. Details about the family background and special qualifications of Martha 'Calamity Jane' Canary, plus her connection with the lady outlaw, Belle Starr, are given in: APPENDIX THREE.

would employ. 'You don't want *strangers* to know what you were *trying* to do. Now do you?'

'No—*NO*!' Ruby admitted, a full realization of the enormity of her behaviour striking her and, twisting into Belle's arms to bury her face against the black habit, she burst into tears.

'There, there!' the lady outlaw soothed, wondering what turn of events could have caused the well dressed and respectable looking young woman to attempt suicide, particularly in such a public and potentially messy fashion. 'I think you had better come with me to somewhere we can talk.'

'B—But I'm n—not a Ca—Catholic,' Ruby objected, looking up.

'And neither am I,' Belle replied, which was true enough even though the rest of her statement was not. 'I belong to a Protestant order. Come along.'

'All right, folks,' Calamity said, swinging around and looking in a prohibitive fashion at the people who were moving forward and talking excitedly amongst themselves. 'It's all over 'n' done with, so let's leave it that way.'

'Is she all right?' a man inquired.

'Sure,' the red head replied, then glanced along the street.

Having brought the stagecoach to a halt, Michael Gilhooley was springing down from his seat on the right side of the driving box. The expression on his face indicated he was both shaken and infuriated by the narrowly avoided accident. After having made the sign of the cross, grasping his long-handled, long-lashed whip in his right fist, he stalked forward with his face suffused by rage. Seeing him coming and taking note of his demeanour, even those onlookers who did not know how uncertain his temper became when he was aroused read the signs and parted to let him through.

'And just what the *hell* kind of game is it you reckon you were playing?' the driver bellowed furiously in a broad Irish brogue, catching Ruby by the shoulder and pulling her away from Belle.

'Take it *easy*, feller!' Calamity snapped, before the young woman she had saved could reply.

'And who the hell was it asking *you* to be pushing your nose in?' Gilhooley demanded. Releasing Ruby, who twisted back into Belle's arms,he swung around to raise the whip in a menacing gesture. Having caught only a fleeting glimpse of the red head while the rescue was taking place, he had noticed her masculine attire and was now too enraged to give the slightest consideration to her gender, 'Mind you own affairs, or it's getting busted it'll be!'

Which, as anybody who knew Calamity could have warned, was not the kind of attitude to take with her at the best of times. While generally good natured, generous to a fault and possessed of a lively sense of humour, it was not her way – particularly when considering she was in the right – to let herself be put upon or abused. What is more, having come through a dangerous and trying situation, she was even less inclined to accept the words and threatening behaviour from the person in part responsible for it. Jumping away from Belle and Ruby, she halted nearer the centre of the street and with a clear space around her in which to take action should it prove necessary. Bringing the bull whip from its belt loop swiftly, she caused its long lash to uncoil behind her with the deft ease which told of much practice.

'You just *try* busting my nose!' the red head declared, standing with feet spread apart and moving her right hand in a way which caused the length of plaited leather to writhe almost as if it possessed a life of its own. 'And my lil friend here'll have *plenty* to say about it!'

'So that's the way of it, huh!' Gilhooley growled, as he ran his gaze over the girl from top to toe, an appreciation of the true state of affairs beginning to assail him. Returning his eyes to studying the twin mounds of what were most definitely *not* masculine flesh forced against the neckline of the buckskin shirt, he went on in a puzzled – but only slightly less hostile – tone, 'Hey, you're not a *man*!'

'My momma told me *that* when I was knee high to a frog,' the red head answered, watching the different – yet equally dangerous – type of whip in the driver's hand, and ready to counter any move it made in her direction. 'Top of which, 'bout the same time, she telled me *never* to run a six-hoss team 'n' wagon lickety-split through a town where folks was walking about.'

'Well now,' the driver growled, hearing a rumble of concurrence with the comment coming from the people around and realizing that his attempt at an impressive arrival had been ruined. The thought did nothing to improve his temper. Therefore, although he refrained from any kind of aggressive action, his Irish temperament would not allow him to let it be imagined he had been deterred by a mere woman. 'You're one of *them* as the town's got so many of right now, are you?'

'One of which *them*?' Calamity inquired, having only arrived an hour earlier and knowing nothing more about Topeka's current affairs than that it was in the throes of an election of some kind.

'Them "Votes For *Women*" bunch's are running 'round making god-damned nuisances of themselves,' Gilhooley explained, his tone showing his antipathy to members of the opposite sex who behaved in such a fashion. 'Sure and you *look* like you could be. All dressed up like a man and it's thinking you are that you can be acting like one.'

Watching and listening, Belle did not care for the way in which the situation was developing. Having glanced around while first comforting the young woman, she had drawn some satisfaction from there not being any peace officers on the scene. However, some would quickly put in an appearance if there should be trouble and she had no desire to be questioned by them about her involvement in the incident. With that in mind, she wanted to try to prevent hostilities taking place, and the extensive knowledge of human nature she had acquired as an adjunct to her illicit activities, which mostly involved various types of confidence tricks, offered a possible solution. She too had seen the driver make the sign of the cross and considered, when used in conjunction with the way she was dressed, this offered the means by which she could try and achieve her purpose.

'Just a moment, my son,' Belle put in, gently freeing herself from Ruby and walking between Gilhooley and the red head before the latter would deliver what she knew would be a blistering response calculated to make the situation worse. Noticing the change which came to the driver's face as he ran his gaze over her attire, she concluded her gamble had a chance of paying off. 'There is no reason *whatsoever* for hard words, or threats to this young woman. It was *my* fault the young *lady* started across the street without watching where she was going and needed to be saved.'

'Was that the way of it, sister?' Gilhooley inquired, losing his attitude of aggression and allowing the whip to sink until dangling at his side.

'*Mother Superior,*' the lady outlaw corrected with a cold haughtiness which suggested she considered the term, 'sister', *infra dig* and even *lese*-clergy when addressed to one of a much higher status. Knowing how great an authority members of the Catholic church could exercise over people of their faith, she adopted the tone and attitude to give her disguise an even greater potency. 'She's a novice for our Order and, *naturally* was hurrying to meet *me*.'

'Sure and I'm *sorry*, Mother Superior,' Gilhooley apologised. Memories of the dominance exerted by women in similar positions of authority when he was a child acting as a strong inducement to subservience despite the superiority he always claimed over other members of her sex. 'I wasn't knowing that.'

'Then perhaps you should be *willing* to let bygones be bygones?' Belle hinted, although her tone and demeanour implied the words were more in the nature of a command. Receiving a hurried nod of concurrence from the driver and noticing with approval that Calamity was coiling and returning the whip to its belt loop – a gesture which she saw he had also observed and which was causing him to relax still more – she went on, 'Bless you, my son. Now why don't you take your stagecoach to the depot where I'm sure they're waiting for it, and the passengers will be wanting to praise you for the skilful way you avoided an accident.'

'I'll be doing just that,' Gilhooley agreed and turned to walk away.

'And now, young lady,' Belle said, as she and the red head returned to where Ruby was standing. 'I think you had better come along with us—!'

'But you told me that you're a *Protestant*,' the young woman protested, her religious upbringing having installed a mistrust of everything to do with the Catholic faith and overriding a natural desire to do as she was instructed.

'I didn't say I was any different to anybody else, now did I?' the lady outlaw inquired with a smile. Glancing around, she discovered, as she had expected, the crowd had decided there would be no more dramatic or interesting developments and had started to go about their respective businesses. Still consumed by curiosity and wanting to try and prevent a further attempt at suicide, using some other method, she went on in a more commanding tone, 'Come along.'

'I've got some things to do right now, *Mother Superior*,' Calamity remarked. 'But I'd admire to see you later.'

'Very well, my child,' Belle assented. 'I'm staying at Mrs. Lane's Boarding House, if you know where it is.'

'I reckon I can find it,' the red head declared, filled with admiration for the way in which the lady outlaw was playing the latest character she had created and sharing the interest in why the young woman had behaved in such a way. 'I'll be there in an hour or so.'

* * *

'I really admired the way you stood up to that *man*!'

Hearing a female voice with the accent of a well educated Bostonian coming from her rear as she was strolling along the sidewalk, Calamity Jane decided the words were meant for her. Glancing over her shoulder, although there were other people looking at her with curiosity and interest, she had no difficulty in deciding who had spoken.

About her height, slender to the point of being bony and perhaps ten years older, the woman coming towards the red head had plain features which were not given even the moderate amount of makeup acceptable for one classed 'good' by the standards of the day anywhere west of the Mississippi River. She had what could have been a man's flat cap on mousey-brown hair taken back tightly into a bun for an effect as unflattering as the rest of her attire. Of excellent quality, there was a masculine cut about her black two-piece travelling outfit and her plain white blouse was adorned by a man's tie.

'Shucks,' Calamity replied, hesitating for a couple of seconds before accepting the right hand thrust towards her. Feeling it tighten on her own, she could not resist the temptation to squeeze back and, on seeing a look of pain mingled with some other emotion she could not decipher, she released her hold. 'Us drivers allus cut loose a mite when we're het up.'

'Are you the *driver* of a stagecoach?' the woman asked with open admiration, retaining her hold until the red head's hand was drawn free.

'Hell, *no*!' Calamity denied, and pride in her occupation caused her to make an explanation even though she felt vaguely uneasy in the other's presence. 'I did *once*, not that I'd want it *known*,[3] 'cause I handle a Conestoga freight wagon for Dobe Killem full-time and I've got to get going and see about 'tending to it.'

'That is *marvellous*!' the woman enthused, falling into step alongside the red head. 'Becoming a *driver*, I mean.'

'It's just a chore,' Calamity claimed off-handedly, feeling puzzled by her not particularly welcome companion's attitude and obvious desire for her company. The majority of 'good' women with whom she came into contact, especially those from the east, disapproved of her way of life and adoption of masculine clothing. 'And it sure beats 'n' pays a whole heap better'n anything else I could be doing.'

'That's *very* true,' the woman declared, putting a hand on the red head's bicep and squeezing gently as if to test its size and firmness. 'There are so *few* kinds of employment

3. *Told in:* CALAMITY SPELLS TROUBLE.

men leave open to *us*. By the way, I'm Linda Bell.'

'Howdy,' the girl said, but ignored the right hand thrust her way. Wondering if the interest was caused by the highly coloured stories about her which she had heard were circulating in the East, she was disinclined to supply her sobriquet in case it increased the eagerness for her company. 'The name's Martha Jane Canary.'

'Call me "Bell",' the woman requested, pouting a little over the refusal to respond to her gesture. 'Do the *men* object to you being a driver, *Canary*?'

'Only happen I run a wheel over their foot,' Calamity answered, deciding she disliked her surname even more now she had heard it expressed in such a fashion.

'Do you *often*—?' the woman began in what seemed to be a hopeful tone. Then she went on in a tone of disapproval. 'Oh, you're only *joking*!'

'I'd hate like hell not to be,' Calamity replied and, in the hope of being able to part company with her unwelcome companion, gestured to an alley they were passing. 'Well, I have to go down *this* way.'

'I hope I can meet you *again*, Canary,' Bell declared, following the red head into the gap between the buildings and once more putting a hand on her sleeve. 'In fact, I'm sure you would *enjoy* the group I'm in town with for the election. We're the "Women's Rights Movement" and it's our purpose to ensure women have *complete* equality with men in *everything*. The others would be delighted to meet you and have you address them on your experiences.'

'Well now,' Calamity said, considering there was nothing she wanted less than to meet with such a group. While of a sturdy and independent nature which made her willing and able to meet men on their own terms in many ways, she was far from being a rampant feminist and, in fact, had never even heard the term. Therefore, she was quite content to accept there were several things they could do which were beyond the abilities of any member of her gender. What was more, from what she had seen of others of her sex expressing a similar point of view to that of Linda Bell, she considered they did more harm than good for the rest of womankind with their attitudes and behaviour. 'I'm not much of a talker.'

'We don't just *talk*, my dear,' Bell said in a conspiratorial fashion, moving around until confronting the red head and placing both hands on her arms. 'In fact, we have quite a lot of *fun* together.'

With a sensation like being struck by an icy deluge, the realization of what was implied by Bell's last sentence came to Calamity. Because of the circumstances in which she had grown up, her conventional education was lacking and, in any case, such things were not included on the curriculum of schools in those days. However, she was far from being naive and unworldly. While she had never encountered such a person until that moment, from what she had heard said by the rest of Cecil 'Dobey' Killem's drivers and other acquaintances of both sexes – none of whom had such inclinations and all of whom considered those who had to be most undesirable company – she was aware that homosexuality existed and was not purely the province of the male gender. Although far from being a prude, like any normal person on finding herself faced by it for the first time, she felt a flood of revulsion.

'So I'll tell the rest of the group you'll come,' Bell continued, before any reply could be made. Running her arms over the sleeves of Calamity's buckskin shirt, that and the rest of the masculine attire made her feel sure the red head must wear such clothing to flaunt a disdain for convention, and also shared her sexual proclivities. She thrust her face closer, 'I have to get back now myself, but I'll come and fetch you tonight if you say where. And, before we part, surely you'll give me a little smack.'

'That's just what I'll do,' Calamity agreed, glancing through the mouth of the alley and deriving satisfaction from there being nobody in sight.

Shrugging herself free from the bony hands, the red head took a step back. Knotting her right fist, she swung it with the skill and precision acquired and improved during numerous brawls which had originated in saloons when the female employees objected to her trespassing upon what they considered as being their domain. Caught at the side of the jaw with a punch powered by a muscular development hard work had strengthened to well beyond the average, Bell was pitched backwards to collide against and slide down the wall of the building at the left. Seated on the ground, her eyes glassy, she looked up into the furious face of her assailant and, despite her wits spinning, was able to hear and understand what was said.

'Our trails aren't likely to cross again,' Calamity declared and, indicative of her feelings, she was telling herself mentally that what she wanted most at that moment was to change the shirt which the woman had pawed and take a bath. 'But, happen they do, don't you come anywheres close to me, you god-damned lesbo, or I'll do a whole lot worse than just give you a *lil smack*!'

* * *

'I've always heard tell most of her sort are that way,' Belle Boyd remarked, having listened with some amusement to a sulphurous description of the meeting with Linda Bell given by Calamity Jane as soon as they were in the room she was occupying at Mrs. Lane's boarding house. Because she knew the owner had a habit – no pun intended – of paying unexpected calls, she was still wearing her disguise. Nevertheless, she contrived to lounge with an almost cat-like grace on the bed. 'In fact, I was told this particular crowd are like it by the girl you saved from being run down by the stage.'

Sitting with legs astride a chair at the dressing-table and resting her arms along the top of its back, the red head wore a tartan shirt and a pair of Levi's pants which had the cuffs of the legs turned up a couple of inches. Both conformed to her physical contours so snugly they gave the impression of having been bought a size too small and shrunk still more during washing. Although the rendezvous with the lady outlaw was in a respectable part of the city, the whip rode in its loop at her waist. She had accepted the prohibition on wearing firearms within the city limits during the period of the election, but was disinclined to have no weapon of any kind on her person.

After parting company with Calamity, Belle had taken Ruby Wakefield to a small coffee-house where they had attracted no attention while they talked. Showing none of her earlier reluctance to accept the 'nun' as a confidant, the young woman had supplied her name and explained that losses she had sustained gambling were responsible for her behaviour. Saying she would do everything possible to help Ruby out of the predicament, Belle had not explained how she intended to go about it. Nor had she mentioned that she considered she would need the support of Calamity if she was to carry out the scheme she had in mind. Instead, she had discovered Ruby was on friendly terms with a sufficiently wealthy family to make one part of her scheme possible. The willingness of the young woman to carry out the instructions was a tribute to the way in which the lady outlaw had built up her confidence and she had shown no hesitation before promising there would be no further attempt to kill herself.

Having accompanied Ruby to the expensive hotel where she was staying and where, in fact, she had made the acquaintance with the cause of her problems, Belle had had a letter written to the leader of the group saying the money to cover the promisory notes signed for the amount of her losses would be procured and handed over in exchange for them that evening in the dining-room. She had dismissed as unimportant the warning that there was no chance of the money being available for the payment, saying all that mattered was the suggestion that payment would be forthcoming was made. She also explained that the young woman should not be in the hotel all evening, and she was assured this would be the case. Before returning to her own accommodation, having learned enough to know what would be needed, the lady outlaw made a purchase which caused the owner of the cigar store in the lobby to give her a puzzled look. Making no attempt to satisfy his obvious curiosity over why a 'nun' would want three decks of cards with backs specially designed to advertize the hotel, she had taken them to her room at Mrs. Lane's boarding house and spent the time while waiting for the red head to join her making them ready for use.

When Calamity had arrived, seeing the obvious disapproval shown by Mrs. Lane, Belle had explained in an aside deliberately pitched just loud enough to be heard by her guest, that she had been asked to come because she was a 'brand to be plucked from the burning and taught the error of her ways'; a statement which prevented any objections to them going to the room. After telling her hostess what she thought of the way she had been described, which both had considered amusing even if Calamity's comment did not appear to express appreciation, the red head was too filled with indignation over her encounter with Linda Bell to leave mentioning it until after being informed of what the lady outlaw had learned.

Although Belle had felt certain Calamity would be a willing ally in any case, albeit probably far from satisfied with the part she was assigned, the meeting with Linda Bell had assured her co-operation was even more whole-hearted!

'Her name's Ruby Wakefield,' the lady outlaw continued her explanation about the girl who had tried to kill herself. 'Seems her daddy's picked up plenty of money out of selling supplies to miners further west. Made sure she had right good schooling – but it missed some of the things a rich girl ought to know and that is why she was acting the way she did when we came across her. She got to know some of that Women's Rights Movement bunch at the hotel where she and they are staying and, figuring they made good sense in what they're saying in the election, if not of the fuss they've been causing at other folks' gatherings, she accepted an invitation to go to what she was told would be a private meeting at a big house in the best part of town. When she arrived, she was smart enough to figure the six of them who were there were only interested in other girls, not fellers, and she was fixing to pull out. But they didn't try to force their attentions on her and one of them suggested a game of cards to pass the time while they was supposed to be waiting for their guest speaker to come to give them a talk.'

'I can close to guess the rest,' Calamity asserted, amused by the cultured southern accent coming from the less than prepossessing appearance which the lady outlaw had given to her otherwise beautiful face. 'But you talk so good, I'll let you tell me.'

'Why thank you 'most to death, you "brand to be plucked from the burning",' Belle replied. 'She thought, them looking so respectable and all, it would be whist, or maybe picquet, but it wasn't. Instead, they told her that draw poker was such a *simple* game, she'd pick it up in no time at all.'

'She picked *something* up, I'll bet!'

'That she did. In fact, she started off winning—!'

'Now that's a real *surprise*!'

'I thought it *might* be,' Belle stated dryly, aware that – while probably not able to match her own knowledge – the red head was well versed in all aspects of gambling. 'Anyways, the game did come easy enough to her. Fact being, although she didn't let on, she'd played it for beads and stuff with her friends at school and home. Seeing as how she was doing so much winning, she didn't notice the stakes were getting higher and higher. Then her *luck* started to change for the worse.'

'And *that's* another *surprise*,' Calamity claimed in an equally sardonic tone.

'Anyways,' the lady outlaw went on. 'It wasn't long before she'd lost all the cash she had to hand and said she was ready to quit. They talked her into just one more hand and, when it was dealt, she knew enough about poker to figure she ought to be able to get at least some of her money back, provided somebody else bet along with her.'

'Which somebody did!'

'Somebody did and they seemed real *obliging*. When she said she didn't have enough money on hand to open, they told her she could sign a note for what she wanted to bet, like some of them had been doing already. So she opened for a couple of hundred, sure she'd get it back and more. Only, at first, it seemed like she'd gone too high and scared the others out. Then the dealer saw her bet and raised it five hundred.'

'That's *real* high!'

'She reckoned having four aces dealt pat made covering it worthwhile. Then, so's the other player wouldn't guess she was holding four of a kind, she figured to play cagey and threw in the spare card to draw one even though it couldn't improve her hand. When the dealer took two, which she reckoned meant drawing to threes and couldn't lick her aces even if the fourth turned up, she was certain she'd got the money and went on to make sure it would be a good enough pile to let her come out a winner.'[4]

'How much of a good pile?'

'All told,' Belle replied sombrely, 'She signed promissory notes for two thousand, five hundred!'

'Whee-dogie!' Calamity ejaculated and, despite the gravity of the situation, she could not resist darting an amused glance at the lady outlaw. 'They took her like Grant took Richmond.'

'Or like Rip Ford took those Yankees at the Battle of Palmitto Hill down back of Brownsville, Texas,' the lady outlaw countered, being an un-Reconstructed Rebel at heart. 'The trouble being, the War had ended almost a month earlier everywhere else.'

'It *never* ended according to *some* folks,' the red head commented, eyeing her hostess in a mock pointed fashion. Then she became serious again and went on, 'So *that's* why she tried to walk under Gilhooley's stage coach?'

'That's only *part* of it,' Belle corrected. 'There was more than just the money she owed made her act that way.'

'What else?' the red head inquired, although her experience with Linda Bell suggested part of the answer.

'They said they'd be willing to forget the notes she signed – provided she'd join them in *everything* they get up

4. An explanation of how the hands rank in the game of poker is given in: TWO MILES TO THE BORDER.

to,' the lady outlaw answered, confirming Calamity's suspicions. 'And, the way I see it, they were wanting to get her in such a bind, should she go along, they'd have had her where they wanted her for the rest of her life, and could bleed her dry by threatening to let her folks and friends know what she'd done to pay off the bet. I've heard their stinking soft-shell kind, men and women alike, have pulled that sort of game before.'

'Those god-damned *bitches*!' the red head spat out furiously, her right hand going to the stock of the whip and wishing it was supplemented by her Navy Colt. 'No wonder she was acting the way she did. Any decent raised gal would be scared *loco* given a stinking choice like *that*. Thing being, Belle, what're *we* going to do about them?'

'You know something, Calamity,' the lady outlaw responded gently, but there was nothing gentle in her expression. 'I thought you'd *never* ask!'

* * *

'All right, ladies,' Belle Boyd said and the disdain in her Southern drawl – which she was deliberately making even more pronounced than usual – was not entirely simulated for the character she was now playing. 'Here we go with a lesson in how to play draw poker Texas' style. Which, happen I don't come out the *winner* in this game, my name's not Betty Hardin. I'm going to take you like my granddaddy, he's *General Ole Devil Hardin*, you know, and his Texas Light Cavalry took those Yankee soldiers in Arkansas all through the War.'[5]

Since the meeting with Calamity Jane at Mrs. Lane's boarding house, the lady outlaw had been very busy!

However, with the time just after eight o'clock in the

5. Information about the campaign against the 'Yankees' waged by General Jackson Baines 'Ole Devil' Hardin and the Texas Light Cavalry is given in various volumes of the Civil War *series.*

evening, Belle was making ready to bring the plan she had outlined to the red head to its climax!

As was suggested by the name she used, the lady outlaw was no longer disguised as a less than attractive looking nun. Making the change had presented no difficulties for her. As an aid to her various confidence tricks, which called for different types of personality to suit the respective needs of the particular role she played, she had caches of clothing and other items in the care of trusted associates at many places throughout the area of her operations.

The store she maintained in Topeka was at the home of an apparently honest businessman who was, nevertheless, a link in a chain for disposing of stolen property which had its centre in the town of Mulrooney.[6] It was only a short distance from the accommodation she had selected for that reason and also because both were in a most respectable part of the State Capital. Choosing what was required, including something supplied by her host, she had set about making the necessary alterations to her appearance. Having taken off the spectacles, removed the bulbous false nose and 'rabbit teeth', she washed away the sallow makeup and allowed her features to revert to their normal beautiful lines. However, for the purposes of her new character, she had given them an expression of imperious arrogance. The habit of the nun was replaced by clothing and jewellery which – in addition to proving her figure was as well endowed as that of Calamity – looked costly, suggesting she was possessed of considerable wealth. To complete the change, she hid her short cropped brunette hair beneath a very realistic black wig coiffured in the latest style.

With the alteration of appearance completed, the lady outlaw had wondered what Elizabeth 'Betty' Hardin – as good a friend as was Calamity Jane in spite of both being completely law abiding – would say if learning of the far from likeable way in which she was to be portrayed in the

6. Further information about this organization is given in: THE CODE OF DUSTY FOG.

interests of getting to know the potential victims and inducing them to respond as was required.[7] Working both on what she had been told by Ruby Wakefield, and by prior experience with their kind, she had put to use the knowledge of human nature so vital to the successful conducting of a confidence trick in selecting a *persona* which would arouse the acquisitive instincts of her quarry. Being aware of the paranoid hostility liberal-radicals of middle class-middle management origins felt towards Southrons, especially those who had been as prominent in the affairs of the former Confederate States as were the genuine Betty Hardin's family, she believed they would be delighted to claim one as a victim. Nor, she felt sure, would they find anything out of the ordinary about the way she intended to behave. It would, in fact, be what they expected from one of her supposed background and upbringing.

Carrying a carpetbag, and wearing a Wavelean hat and with a long yellow 'duster' coat such as was used when travelling over her other attire, Belle had timed her arrival at the hotel, where the members of the Women's Rights Movement were staying, to coincide with their return from disrupting a political meeting. She saw some of them watching her with interest, if not favour, particularly when she had announced loudly in the pronounced Southern drawl that she could and would willingly pay for the *very* best suite. Informed by the desk clerk that there was only one single room available, she had insisted upon making an examination before reaching a decision, and explained away her lack of baggage by stating it had been left at the Wells Fargo depot until she had made sure the accommodation would be up to her requirements.

Having attracted the attention of her quarry at the reception desk, Belle had entered the dining-room at seven o'clock and tried just as loudly to order dishes particularly favoured south of the Mason-Dixon line. She had

7. *For information about Elizabeth 'Betty' Hardin's family background, see:* Footnote 13 *of the* Introduction *to this volume.*

left the hat and 'duster' in the carpetbag – which had held only old newspapers supplied by the man in charge of her cache – and was clad in a mauve silk blouse with puff sleeves and a black velvet skirt which concealed her footwear. To further emphasise her 'wealthy' state, yet supposedly gauche nature, she was wearing a quantity of jewellery which looked most impressive and would have been more suitable for a formal affair than just coming to have a casual evening meal at a hotel. As on her arrival at the reception desk, everything about her appearance and voice was calculated to persuade the women she was after to decide she would be an ideal victim. Therefore, she had not been surprised when she was approached by the one she knew to be their leader.

Coming to Belle's table, Mary Abbott had engaged her in conversation by starting to discuss the rights of women. Declaring she had no interest whatsoever in 'Yankee' politics, she had expressed a wish to do some gambling and, gesturing with the vanity bag she had brought downstairs, claimed it held enough money to support her desire to play for high stakes. Taking the bait, the feminist had told her of a game of draw poker which might prove satisfactory. Stating that she doubted whether she would find any worthwhile competition outside Texas for one of her skill, she had agreed to participate in a manner suggesting she considered she would be doing the other players a favour by competing.

Studying Abbott all the time they were talking, the lady outlaw felt certain the letter from Ruby Wakefield had been accepted at its face value. In her early thirties, tallish, lean and gaunt featured, with her black hair swept back into a bun, the feminist wore a black dress which did nothing to make her more attractive. Clasping a bulky black reticule on the table, she continually darted glances at the entrance to the dining-room and showed signs of annoyance, beyond that caused by the comments 'Betty Hardin' was passing, when the person she was obviously awaiting failed to put in an appearance. Therefore, knowing how best to achieve her purpose, Belle displayed what seemed like impatience to be getting involved in the promised game of poker. Her statement that she believed Abbott was 'running scared' and she would have to look elsewhere for her diversion proved successful. Glaring down at the reticule, the feminist thrust back her chair and said they would get going. Asked if they would be playing in a room at the hotel, she replied that the venue was a mansion loaned by a supporter of the Women's Rights Movement as it offered a greater privacy.

On going to the reception desk, learning Ruby Wakefield had left the hotel earlier and was still absent, Abbott did not return to her room to leave behind the promissory notes which Belle felt sure were in her reticule, and the plan which the lady outlaw had had ready to deal with such a contingency was not required. She only delayed the departure for long enough to place all the jewellery she was wearing in the safe in the manager's office supplied for the benefit of the residents. Then she reappeared with a thick bundle of what appeared to be brand new ten dollar bills, causing an avaricious gleam to come into the feminist's eyes as she placed it in her commodious vanity bag. Having sent her companions to prepare for the game, Abbott took their intended victim to the venue in a hansom cab. What she did not know was that Calamity Jane was following in another which was driven by an acquaintance of Cecil 'Dobey' Killem and who had offered his services for the evening without asking any questions.

The mansion to which Belle was taken stood in its own grounds, surrounded by a high wall. Passing along the wide path to the front entrance, passing through a garden with a number of bushes decorating well cared for lawns, she noticed only one room at the front showed any sign of occupancy. Just beyond where a fair sized cottonwood tree was growing, a light glowed through a set of French windows beyond a balustrade and porch over which was a balcony for the rooms on the unlit second floor. Commenting upon the otherwise deserted aspect of the building, she was told this was because the owners were away on vacation and had given the Women's Rights Movement permission to use it in their absence for holding meetings with sympathisers. Wondering whether this was correct and feeling sure the offer did not include running a dishonest poker game with blackmail as its eventual object, the lady outlaw did not take the matter any further. However, she considered its lack of occupants other than the women against whom she would be in contention and the comparative isolation of the property made it just as well suited to her purpose as theirs.

Passing through the gloomy entrance hall and into the large dining-room, illuminated by two large crystal chandeliers, Belle found the other five members of the group which had cheated Ruby Wakefield were seated at the table in the centre and were trying to give the impression that they had been playing for some time. Studying their behaviour, she concluded it would not have fooled anybody with the slightest experience of crooked gambling. Not, she also reminded herself, that their victims had been in such a category until she had caused herself to be selected.

Making sure she had obtained the seat at the left of Abbott, while being introduced to the others, the lady outlaw had subjected each to a scrutiny and assessment of the respective potential they possessed in what she felt sure would follow. If it did not, she had thought with some amusement, Calamity would be even more disappointed than herself. Judging from their appearances, she could imagine why each had elected to become a feminist and discard association with men. Their hair was done in unflattering styles and their clothes were intended to prevent any suggestion of their figures showing. Not one had an appearance likely to find favour with members of the opposite sex.

If the red head's pungent description had not been sufficient for Belle, the bruise on the jaw of the woman at Abbott's right would have identified her as Linda Bell. Next came the biggest of them, almost six foot tall, bulky and surly faced Merle Amory. Except for one being a blonde and the other a red head, Jill Forbes and Margaret Gascoigne were sufficiently alike in size, build, narrow and sharp, unpleasant features to be Abbott's sisters. About six inches shorter than Amory, Louise Anderson had the build of a badly made plum pudding and the lady outlaw considered she looked nearly as intelligent, which was not saying much.

Noticing all of the women were wearing rings which would make effective weapons when the trouble she anticipated erupted, Belle had caused them to be removed. Claiming that as she had heard of devices being fitted to them as an aid to marking cards, she had deliberately left her own rings behind as an indication of good faith, she insisted that while she felt sure nothing of the kind would be attempted – in a manner which implied she did – she expected the other players to show a similar respect for the game. Despite their protests, seeing she was adamant and being led to assume she would leave the game if not humoured, the feminists did as she wished and placed the rings they took off in their reticules on their laps. However, she had not been able to find a counter when Abbott said the drapes must be drawn across the French windows to prevent anybody seeing the game was taking place. Although this would mean Calamity could not watch what was happening, Belle drew consolation from the night being sufficiently warm for the transom at the top to be left open to allow in a cooling breeze.

Having achieved all she wanted, with the exception of the shades, the lady outlaw was ready to put the remainder of her scheme into operation and made the declaration which she did not doubt would cause the women to be even more determined to get her in their power.

* * *

'Well, that's all the cash I have with me,' Belle Starr announced in a tone suggestive of bitterness. 'So I'm going to finish.'

I haven't been doing so well either,' Merle Amory rumbled in her deep, almost man-like voice. 'So I'll go out and see if there's a hansom we can use to go back to the hotel.'

'Why not have another hand while she's looking, Betty?' Mary Abbott inquired, gathering up and starting to shuffle the cards, as the big woman rose and lumbered away with all the grace of a particularly clumsy hippopotamus.

'I just told you that I don't have any more money with me,' the lady outlaw pointed out sullenly.

'Then do like you've seen some of the other girls do,' Abbott suggested. 'Sign a promissory note and, if you lose, make it good when you get back to the hotel.'

The game of draw poker had gone on for just over an hour. While it was taking place, Belle had satisfied herself she was not up against skilled card manipulators. In fact, had she wished, she could have taken them for all the money they had with them by putting her own training in that field to use. Instead, she had given a most convincing performance of possessing a little ability which was only dangerous to herself. Wondering whether the opposition had sufficient card savvy to appreciate what she was doing, she had sought to convey the impression of one trying to prove herself much more knowledgeable and being better at playing draw poker than was really the case.[8] What was more, to ensure her actions at the appropriate moment did not come as a surprise and arouse comment, she had insisted upon patting the remainder of the deck 'for luck' – using a twisting motion of her left hand to display it was empty – every time before she was given the number of cards she asked to 'draw'.

At first, as had happened when Ruby Wakefield was the victim, the feminists had done everything they could – such as claiming to have been beaten by what was actually an inferior hand – to ensure a suitable frame of mind by allowing their 'unsuspecting victim' to win. Even when they sought to change her 'luck', which was genuinely good and which none possessed the necessary manipulat-

8. How a skilful player performed such a deception is described in: BEGUINAGE.

ive ability to change, on several occasions she had had to discard hands capable of taking the pot if she had gone to a showdown. While being allowed to win, she had acted happy and, to supply a further inducement for the feminists to believe she could be made the subject of blackmail, boasted of how her grandfather, 'General Ole Devil Hardin, you know', had entrusted her with a very large sum of money to deliver to a business associate in Topeka. She had also committed 'errors of judgement' which encouraged them to believe they were achieving their purpose. Playing her part perfectly, when the 'reverses' to her fortunes began to take toll, she had behaved in what seemed to be a more reckless fashion which helped reduce her finances to the point where the completely dishonest ploy could be performed.

'All right, I'll do that,' Belle agreed.

'Put your full name and address at the top, then write I.O.U. and the sum and sign it,' Abbott instructed, fetching a notepad, pen and bottle of ink from a drawer in the sidepiece. 'It's only a formality which is *always* done when playing poker, as you must know, Hard—*Betty.*'

'Why sure, we do it *all* the time back home to Texas,' the lady outlaw answered in the tone of one trying to prove a non-existent experience to match that which she believed the other players possessed. Taking the pen, she wrote, '*Elizabeth Hardin, OD Connected Ranch, Rio Hondo County, Texas*' in a childish scrawl. Then what passed for a crafty expression came to her face and she continued, 'I'll fill the amount in *after* I've seen my cards.'

'Of course,' Abbott agreed. 'Cut the deck and we'll get on with the game.'

'Cut light, lose all night's been working,' Belle said bitterly, splitting the pile of cards well below the halfway point. 'So I'll go deeper this time.'

'Let's hope it improves your luck,' Abbott replied. Directing a pointed glance and nod at Linda Bell, she swung her gaze across the room and went on, 'Why it's Amory back already!'

'Sorry, Hardin!' the biggest of the feminists boomed. 'There isn't a hansom anywhere to be seen.'

Knowing she was expected to fall victim to the distraction, Belle had obligingly looked around even before hearing her 'name'. She had no need to keep Abbott and Bell under observation to know they were changing the cards she had seen shuffled and cut herself for another deck which was suitably prepared supplied from the latter's reticule. Being certain this had happened, without needing to so much as glance down, she dropped her hands into her lap and made the necessary preparations for coping with the situation. Then she sat back with an air of unsuspecting innocence and watched the new cards being dealt.

'I'll put you in, Amory,' Abbott announced. 'Then we'll make this the *last* hand and we'll all go back to the hotel in the carriage you girls used to come out here.'

Paying no attention to the mutter of concurrence from the other feminists, apart from realizing it was to put her in the required mood for what lay immediately ahead, Belle picked up and looked at five cards which would have gladdened the heart of a genuine player in the position she had allowed herself to reach. Keeping up her performance as the pretended authority who was really far from experienced or competent, she allowed the kind of intake of breath she suspected had been given by most of the previous victims at the sight of the four aces she was dealt pat.

'Is there a *limit* to what we can bet?' the lady outlaw inquired with well simulated eagerness.

'Certainly not,' Abbott declared and flickered a glance of triumph at the other feminists.

'I—I'll open for one—three—*five* hundred!' Belle announced, even though aware that the choice should have been with the player at the right of the dealer and progress around the others before she spoke. Laying down the cards and grabbing the pen, she continued excitedly, 'I'll fill in the rest of the amounts on the promissory note as I bet them.'

'That's fine with us,' Abbott asserted as the writing was

commenced, also disregarding the correct order of betting in her eagerness to get the better of the beautiful Southern girl who had aroused her envy and hatred for having attributes she lacked. Directing another triumphant look at her companions and starting to count out the money, she added, 'I'll see you and raise you five hundred!'

'That's *far* too much for *me*, Abbott!' Bell claimed, tossing her cards to the centre of the table.

'And me,' Amory grunted, repeating the disposal. 'I might just as well not have joined in again.'

'I'm out,' Jill Forbes declared.

'And me,' Margaret Gascoigne supported.

'Not with what I've got,' Louise Anderson stated, also throwing her hand into the discards. 'It looks like it's left between just you two, Hardin, Abbott.'

'So it does,' Belle agreed, with what passed as relief that she had opposition to benefit her very powerful hand. 'I'll see that five hundred and raise it the same.'

'You must have *good* cards!' Abbott commented, almost sounding as if she did not know the exact value of the hand held by her intended victim. Pushing forward the appropriate amount from the money before her, she went on, 'Well, so have I and I believe that if you have them, play them. I'll have to see that five. How many cards do you want?'

'Two,' the lady outlaw answered, tossing the ace of spades and nine of clubs face down among the discards with a well produced smirk of triumph.

'Don't you want to pat the cards for luck?' Abbott inquired with just a hint of mockery and, showing no signs of surprise at the decision, refrained from picking up the unused portion of the deck.

'Wha—Oh *yes*, of course!' Belle ejaculated, having taken up the pen with her right hand as if impatient to carry on betting. Reaching out, still conveying the impression of being wanting to resume the game and collect the winnings she anticipated, she tapped the remainder of the deck without having first made the twisting motion which she had done previously to establish her left palm was empty. Snatching it back, as soon as she received the top two cards and looked at them, she continued, 'I'll open for five hundred!'

'You definitely *must* have improved your hand,' Abbott commented and again sent a smirk of satisfaction around the table. 'I'll take two as well. Perhaps we're both after the same thing?'

'It could be,' Belle drawled and glanced at the drapes across the French windows. Still simulating the eagerness of one convinced she had the winning hand, she went on, 'Well, what are you going to do?'

'How much are you willing to go for?' Abbott inquired, without troubling to examine the two cards she gave herself.

Once before when using the ploy, the intended victim had evidently heard of it and sought to nullify the effect by discarding an ace and the fifth card. However, the man from whom Abbott had learned of the trick had warned this might happen and supplied a counter for such attempts at nullification. When preparing the deck, she gave herself the nine, ten, jack of hearts and two valueless cards. However, on top of the remainder were the seven, eight, queen and king of hearts to take care of any contingency. Generally the victim would draw one card, hoping to make it appear she was trying to fill a flush or straight. In which case, the eight and queen would supply a straight flush. If she tried as had 'Betty Hardin' to completely ruin the ploy by taking two, the queen and king would still be available to produce the powerful hand which would even have beaten the four aces.

'I can cover everything on the table, yours and theirs, with the money I was given to pay off—I left at the hotel,' the lady outlaw claimed. 'Why not get them to loan you theirs and we'll have a showdown for it all?'

'Why not?' Abbott agreed, noticing the way the first part of the comment was amended and delighted by the possibilities for blackmail she felt sure were being offered. 'If they don't mind lending me their money, that is?'

'You can have mine,' Bell confirmed and, being equally aware of what was to come despite the attempt of the 'Texan' to circumvent the ploy, the other four were just as eager to comply.

'That comes to fifteen hundred dollars,' Abbott announced, showing no concern over the money she was using being the funds supplied by the people sponsoring the Women's Rights Movement for attending the election and disrupting opposition politicians. 'And, with what you've already bet, you'll be signing the promissory note for over two thousand.'

'That's all right with me,' Belle declared with complete truth. 'And, while I'm writing out the promissory note, will you separate the new bills I brought so nobody will get to know I've used the—so I can put them back—! I mean, it will save time when I w—!'

'Don't worry, we *know* what you mean,' Abbott replied, more convinced than ever that the loss of the money entrusted to 'Betty Hardin's' care anticipated by all the feminists would put her completely in their power and savoring the humiliations they would heap upon her. 'We'll only be too pleased to do *everything* we can for *you*.'

'Well, that's *that*!' the lady outlaw asserted, having taken sufficient time for the separation to be completed while filling in the designated sum of money beneath the name and address she had supplied. 'Let's play poker!'

'What do you have?' Abbott inquired, wanting to make the beautiful Southern girl suffer as much as possible when the showdown took place.

'Full house, aces and tens!' Belle replied, turning her cards face up on the table and starting to whistle 'Dixie' loudly.

'Fu—?' Abbott gurgled and snatched up her own cards for the first time since completing the draw. To her horror, instead of the expected queen and king of hearts, to provide a straight flush and defeat the full house which should not be confronting her, she found she had replaced the two valueless cards from her hand with the four of clubs and six of spades for a 'jack high' and, under the unexpected circumstances, completely worthless hand. 'I—I—I shouldn't have *these* two—!'

'Now how would a player in a *honest* game know *that*?' the lady outlaw asked in her normal tone, having stopped the whistling and tensed on her seat.

The difference in the way 'Betty Hardin' spoke while posing the question brought every eye from the exposed cards to her. Considering the benefits in upbringing and education each had been given by their respectively indulgent middle class-middle management parents, which had imbued little more than an over-inflated sense of what was actually non-existent personal superiority and brilliance, not one of the feminists could be termed bright or particularly perceptive. However, all of them were able to discern the change which had come over their intended victim. The realization that her earlier naive behaviour had been nothing more than a successful pose, adopted to outwit and turn the tables on them, came almost simultaneously. That it was achieved by a woman with such obviously Southern origins and who had the beauty and physical attractions they lacked and envied, while pretending to despise such attributes, made the discovery even more galling for each of them.

'She's *tricked* us!' Bell screeched, shoving back her chair and starting to stand up while pointing an accusatory finger at Belle.

'The peckerwood bitch *knew* what to *expect*!' Amory said at the same moment, watching the lady outlaw starting to thrust their money—but not the new bills—into her vanity bag.

'She had cards *palmed* and put them on the deck when she touched it for *luck*!' Abbott assessed correctly, the four having been extracted without detection earlier and retained beneath the vanity bag on Belle's lap. 'Come on, girls. Let's teach her a *lesson* she'll *never* forget!'

'There's only one thing I can say to *that*!' Belle declared mockingly, using sufficient force in thrusting back her chair to ensure she was able to rise and move away from the table without impediment. As the rest of the feminists also began to come to their feet and move towards her, tossing the now bulging vanity bag on to the sidepiece near a bowl containing artificial fruit, she raised her voice in a yell. 'Hey, *CALAMITY*!'

* * *

Seeing the drapes being drawn at the french windows while she was advancing cautiously through the bushes towards the mansion, Calamity Jane had shared Belle Starr's misgivings. Taking advantage of the occupants being unable to look outside, she had crossed the porch and gently tried the handles. Finding the lock and bolts were secured, she had realized the disadvantage she was facing. Glancing around, she decided there was a way in which she might be able to see what was happening and be ready to lend the assistance she had agreed upon with the lady outlaw when the climax of the game was reached. Although the rest of the lower branches had been removed, one sufficiently sturdy to support a children's swing was left on the cottonwood tree just beyond the balustrade. It was parallel to the house and at a sufficient height for her to be able to keep watch through the uncovered and open transom. Climbing up, aided by the ropes of the swing, had proved easy enough and was accomplished without making enough noise to be heard inside the dining-room.

Standing on the limb and finding she was able to see most of the table at which the game would take place, the red head had watched the feminists being compelled to remove and put away their rings. The sight gave her satisfaction. Until meeting the lady outlaw, she had been anticipating a boring visit to Topeka. Because of the delicate state of affairs caused by the election, being all too aware of her penchant for becoming involved in brawls and other unruly incidents, her employer had given orders that she must keep out of trouble.

Watching the game commence, Calamity was pleased with the way things had turned out. Knowing he was a firm believer in justice being done– even if not in a strictly legal fashion – she was convinced Dobey Killem would approve of what she was doing should he hear about it. There was certain to be physical opposition when the truth about 'Betty Hardin' was revealed and she was looking forward to tangling with the women who had almost caused Ruby Wakefield to commit suicide. Studying them, despite realizing they would have the advantage of numbers on their side, she had felt no qualms over having being compelled to leave her gunbelt and Navy Colt behind. When the time came, she told herself as she squatted on her haunches to await developments, there would be the satisfaction of dealing out punishment with her bare hands and any other way required in excess of that already inflicted upon Bell.

Rising to her feet at intervals, Calamity had kept the progress of the game under observation. Although she was seated when the 'distraction' allowed Mary Abbott to change the decks, hearing 'Dixie' being whistled and knowing only the lady outlaw would select that particular tune, caused her to get up. Having already decided how to make her entrance, she balanced herself on the branch and started to put the idea into effect. Bringing the whip from its belt loop, she caused the lash to uncoil behind her and sent it forward and upwards. By the kind of coincidence no author of fiction would dare employ in a plot, Belle yelling her name came at the same instant as the explosive crack of the lash and prevented it from being heard by the feminists.

While giving the shout for assistance, the lady outlaw was also making ready for action on her own behalf. To facilitate doing so, she put to use a modification to her attire which she had learned from another good and law abiding woman friend, Belle 'the Rebel Spy' Boyd.[9] Giv-

9. Information about the career of Belle 'the Rebel Spy' Boyd is given in: Footnote 11 *of the* Introduction *to this volume.*

ing a tug at the fastening of the waistband, she caused it to open out. Set free, the black velvet skirt fell downwards to show she had on brown riding breeches and boots instead of conventional feminine undergarments and footwear. Stepping clear, she lashed around a backhand blow to the face which spun Mary Abbott away from her. However, she felt herself grabbed by the shoulder from behind. Before she could retaliate, Louise Anderson gave her a surging shove and she was propelled in a sprawl against the sidepiece. A glance to her rear warned that her assailant and the other feminists were moving in her direction.

Curling out as directed, the end of the whip's lash wrapped around the top of the guardrail for the upstairs' balcony. Giving a tug to ensure it was sufficiently tight for her needs, Calamity grasped the handle in both hands and, first jumping to the rear, launched herself from her perch. Swinging downwards, under the impulsion of the pendulous effect her weight gave to the tightly stretched and strong plaited leather, she lifted her legs so they passed over the top of the porch's balustrade. Arriving with the full force of her shapely and powerful body behind them, her feet struck the framework where the two parts of the French windows came together. The impact burst them inwards to the accompaniment of splintering wood and breaking glass. Having released the handle, she plummeted onwards into the room and alighted in a kneeling posture with arms thrown behind her as an aid to retaining balance.

Hearing the commotion, all the feminists came to a halt and looked around. Linda Bell realized the newcomer was the red head with whom she had tried to become more than just casually acquainted instead of continuing her task of following to make sure Ruby Wakefield did not go to lodge a complaint with the local peace officers. Aroused by the thought of how she was spurned when she had made the proposition, she gave a screech like a scalded cat. Forgetting what had happened, she rushed across the room with her hands extended to grab hair. It was not, anybody who knew her proposed victim could have warned, the wisest or most effective action she could have carried out.

Thrusting herself towards the approaching feminist, Calamity did not straighten from the crouching posture. Instead, her head passed beneath the reaching fingers and rammed into Bell's midsection. Thrown backwards with all the air driven from her lungs, the stricken woman folded at the waist and dropped to her knees. However, as she went, Margaret Gascoigne had concluded the newcomer was not there by chance nor to aid the cause of the Women's Rights Movement and, electing to leave dealing with 'Betty Hardin' to the others, was dashing to the attack.

Snatching up the bowl of artificial fruit from near her vanity bag, Belle twisted around and flung its contents into Anderson's face. Having done so, she gave her attention to the next nearest of her intended assailants. Taking a warning from what happened to Abbott, Jill Forbes allowed Amory to pass her. Lumbering up, the massive woman hurled a punch at the lady outlaw. However, while the fist was propelled by all her weight and undoubted power, it was slow and 'telegraphed' to one with Belle's considerable experience in such matters. Swivelling onwards from dealing with Anderson, she deftly interposed the sturdy metal bowl so it and not her face was struck by the approaching knuckles. A yelp of pain burst from Amory and, before she could recover from the shock, a foot was rammed against her stomach to thrust her backwards. Despite having removed the biggest of the feminists, Belle was not to be given a respite. Abbott, Anderson and Forbes were all converging upon her.

Straightening up, Calamity caught Gascoigne by the wrist and, stepping aside, gave a swinging heave which propelled her across the room. Then, seeing Belle was about to be attacked by the three feminists, she set about rendering assistance. Darting forward, she bounded on to and dived across the table. Flying through the air, she threw an arm around the necks of Abbott and Forbes while passing between them. Coming down on her feet, causing her captives to reel and bend at the waist, she sought to retain her hold long enough for the lady outlaw to deal with the third would-be attacker and take action against them.

Ignoring her companions' problems, Anderson sent her fingers into what she imagined to be stylishly coiffured black hair and gave a savage jerk at it. However, the attack did not meet the response she anticipated. Before she could realize the locks she was grasping were artificial, they came away in her hands without causing the recipient of the attack either pain or inconvenience. In fact, the only one to suffer from it was Anderson. Caught by a roundhouse punch to the jaw which proved her assailant to be as competent as the red haired intruder, letting the wig fall from her hands as she went, she was sent in a twirling sprawl across the room.

Realizing she would need covering for her head and wanting to keep the wig from being damaged, Belle kicked it under the sidepiece before doing anything else. Then, turning, she found Calamity was still holding Abbott and Forbes in the side head-locks. Struggling to get free from the choking grip, they were pulling her head back by its shortish red locks and digging fingers into the inside of her thighs in what – despite the sturdy blue material of the Levi's pants – was obviously an equally painful fashion. In fact, the punishment they were inflicting had the desired effect, if not quite as they would have wished. Letting out a pungent profanity, Calamity gave a surging upwards heave and removed her arms to send the pair away from her in a spinning stumble. Advancing to help the red head, Belle interlocked her fingers and swung them to catch Forbes at the side of the jaw. Although she knocked the feminist staggering, as she was about to follow up the blow, Amory was rushing at her. Bending at the waist before the outstretched hands could sieze her, she straightened as the biggest feminist collided against her and tipped forward. Made to perform an involuntary half somersault over her intended victim, Amory descended with a thud upon the thick carpet covering the floor.

The fight raged with unabated fury for over five minutes. Throughout it, superiority in numbers was all the feminists had in their favour. Driven by fury and a mutual desire to take revenge upon the Southern girl who had made such fools of them, their efforts were completely without cohesion and they got in one another's way to the benefit of their opponents. What was more, they were up against two women in the peak of physical condition and who respectively possessed considerable knowledge of wrestling, fist fighting and all-in brawling.

There was not a second when fists and feet were still instead of being used with complete impartiality. In addition, hair was grabbed at and pulled. However, although the shortish locks of Calamity and Belle were far less susceptible than those of their antagonists – particularly as the buns disintegrated – generally they preferred more effective methods of attack. Almost incessantly, whether from their punches, kicks, pushes, or a variety of wrestling throws, one or another of the the feminists was sent staggering and sprawling, or flipped through the air to alight with varying degrees of impact. Clutching fingers damaged clothes, but the attire of the opposition offered far greater scope than the more snugly fitting garments worn by Belle and Calamity. All had their blouses torn to varying degrees and not one of the feminists' skirts survived undamaged. Pulled from the waistband of the Levi's pants, in addition to having all the buttons ripped off, the red head's shirt lost a sleeve.

Not everything went in favour of the red head and Belle. At times one, the other, or both were in difficulties. However, on each occasion, the skill possessed by whichever was in trouble helped her to escape, or her friend came to her assistance. Therefore, as a result of their individual and combined efforts, aided by the ineptitude of the feminists – all of whom were engaged for the first time in physical conflict – at last Calamity and the lady outlaw were getting the better of the fracas.

Moving forward to attack Belle, who was caught around the arms from behind by Forbes, Gascoigne was thwarted. Bringing up her feet, the lady outlaw rammed them into the red haired feminist's chest and gave a thrust which caused the blonde to stagger and let go. Precipitated backwards and losing her balance, Gascoigne went down with her head cracking against the sidepiece hard enough to render her *hors de combat*. She was the first of her group to be put out of action by only a slight margin. Pivoting fast, Belle brought off an uppercut which took Forbes under the chin and knocked her out as effectively as her predecessor. She crashed spread-eagled on the floor.

Having lost her skirt, bringing into view long legged white cotton knickers and spindly calves, Linda Bell was shoved on to the table by Anderson who was trying to get at Belle. Coming to her feet, she saw Calamity was being punched in the stomach by Amory.

'How do *you* like being hit in the gut!' the red head yelled, twisting at the torso and delivering a much more effective blow.

As the fist sank almost wrist deep into her midsection, if the reaction from Amory was any guide, she did not like it. Her eyes and cheeks bulged out as all the air was driven from her lungs in a belching squawk. Clutching at the point of impact with both hands, she collapsed winded and helpless to her knees. At the sight of her particular friend being treated in such a fashion, especially as it was done by the red head she already had cause to hate, Linda Bell screeched and threw herself bodily from the table. More by chance than deliberately, she tilted sideways with the intention of crashing into and knocking Calamity face down to the floor. However, the yell had been an error in tactics and the red head swung around instead of being caught from the rear. What was more, as the slender body arrived against her torso, she had the weight and strength to withstand the hoped for effect.

Before Linda Bell could drop to the floor, she was grabbed by the throat with Calamity's right hand and the other was slipped between her thighs to grasp the waistband of her knickers. Deftly twisting her writhing captive from hortizontal to vertical, the red head turned and stepped to where Amory was still kneeling and showing the distress caused by the punch to the stomach. Raising Linda Bell, undeterrred by her wildly waving arms and legs, Calamity swung her downwards so the top of her head slammed against that of the biggest feminist. Rendered unconscious, Amory keeled over backwards and, on being released, Bell flopped down to alight supine and just as flaccidly across her bulky torso.

Having put two more of the feminists out of the fight, tackled around the waist by Abbott, Calamity was brought down. They went rolling across the floor struggling furiously, to end with the red head's legs wrapped around and crushing at the leader of the group's head. Retaining the scissor-hold, despite the writhing and kicking its recipient was doing in an attempt to escape, Calamity looked around. Not too far away, Belle and Anderson had their fingers interlocked and they were engaged in an instinctive trial of strength. What was more, having contrived to take a less active part in the conflict than her companions, Anderson was able to match the strength of the lady outlaw. In fact, because of the exertions to which Belle had been subjected, she was finding herself in something close to a stalemate.

Glancing around while continuing the constriction she was applying to Abbott's head, Calamity decided to help the lady outlaw. Opening her ledgs, she rolled away from her captive to grab and jerk at Anderson's ankles. Alarmed by the attack, the bulky feminist could not help relaxing the efforts she was making with her arms. Snatching her hands free, Belle lashed up her right leg. Anderson's skirt had been torn down the front and was flapping open, so the foot had nothing to impede it as it rose between her thighs and struck the bottom of her knickers.

Although her assailant had been unable to attain the power which could have been employed earlier in the fight, she clasped at the vulnerable point of her anatomy and, doubling at the waist, turned away gasping in pain.

Taking advantage of Calamity being distracted, Abbott began to rise with the intention of running from the room. She was not allowed to carry out her plan. Instead of following up the attack on Anderson, Belle darted over to grab the leader of the group by her sweat matted and tangled black hair. Jerked erect, Abbott received a punch in the stomach which folded her at the middle. Then her head was grabbed and encircled by the lady outlaw's left arm. While this was happening, Calamity had got up and caught Anderson in the same fashion. Converging at a run and dragging their captives after them, they caused the tops of the protruding heads to be rammed together with a click like two giant billiard balls making contact. Jolted free by the collision, Abbott and Anderson toppled on to their backs and, after each's body had writhed spasmodically for a moment, went limp.

* * *

'L—Looks like they're *all* plump tuckered out,' Calamity Jane gasped, glancing around and sounding just a trifle disappointed.

'L—Looks that way,' Belle Starr confirmed, after sucking in a few deep breaths. Studying the sprawled out feminists, all of whom had either bloody noses or other injuries acquired in the conflict, she went on, 'Your face is a mite redder than usual, but it's not marked up like some of them are. How about me?'

'You've come through it without getting more than a touch mussed up,' the red head assessed. 'What now?'

'I want to take a look in Abbott's bag,' Belle replied. 'Will you collect all the cards we were using.'

'Sure,' the red head assented and, starting to do as she was told, went on, 'How about this money?'

'Leave the new stuff,' the lady outlaw answered and went to pick up Abbott's reticule. Opening the envelope she extracted, she looked at the contents. 'I thought she'd have Ruby Wakefield's promissory notes with her, but this's even *better.*'

'How come?' Calamity asked, without interrupting the task of gathering the cards used in the final hand and the money belonging to the feminists which Belle had not had time to put in her reticule.

'She's got the rest they've tricked other girls into signing with her,' the lady outlaw explained, guessing correctly that Abbott had been too mistrusting to leave such items in the safe at the hotel. Picking up the pen, notepad and inkwell which had been knocked to the floor along with the cards and money during the fighting, she found there was still enough ink left for her purpose. 'I'm leaving them a warning that I'm sending the notes to the girls who've been slickered saying they should put the law on them. Likely none of the girls will want to let it be found out what happened, so won't do it; but Abbott and her crowd are going to be as worried as hell in case one or more of them should do it.'

'They deserve to be more than just *worried*, but we'll likely have to settle for just that,' Calamity declared. 'Anyways, I've got all the cards. What now?'

'You'll find three decks in my vanity bag,' Belle replied. 'Throw one over the floor like those you picked up were and put the others into this bag of Abbott's.'

'Yo!' the red head assented. 'Mind telling me why?'

'I'm going to have Mick tell the first lawman he sees that he heard a ruckus here and, knowing the folks who own it are away, reckons it should be looked into.'

'That's smart figuring, but why'd we need to change the cards?'

'Happen the lawman we send looks careful, which I reckon he will, he'll find they're *marked*. I've made sure of *that*. Then he's going to start asking questions that could delay him getting somebody to come after us.'

'It's your game and I'll play it out, even if we *both* wind up in the pokey,' Calamity declared. 'But it seems a pity to leave them all this money.'

'You'd be likely to wind up "in the pokey" if you took it and tried to spend it,' the lady outlaw replied, waving the sheet of paper upon which she had written to dry the ink. 'They're all *forgeries* I bought cheap for the game.'

'There's only one lil thing,' Calamity commented, as the other preparations for departure were being completed. Anticipating there would be a fight, she had not brought her kepi and was doing what she could to make her damaged shirt presentable for being viewed outside the building. Having replaced the discarded skirt, Belle was donning the wig retrieved from beneath the sidepiece. 'I know it's only 'til you can get to the bag you gave me to bring along and ole Mick won't say nothing, 'though I reckon he'll *enjoy* the view, but you'll sure have anybody's might see us leaving looking at you kind of *curious* and, way this high-toned end of town'll be watched over, that lawman you're wanting could be one of them.'

'Well now,' Belle replied, aware the blouse and silk shift beneath it had been torn so badly they could no longer conceal her bosom. 'I'd *never* have thought of that. Come on, I saw the bunch who were here when I arrived had left their hats and coats on the stand by the front door and I'll use one of them.'

Glancing around and satisfying themselves that none of the feminists were showing signs of recovery, Calamity and the lady outlaw left the room. Crossing the entrance hall, Belle collected a shawl from the attire put on the stand by the women who had meant to cheat her. Wrapping it around her shoulders, she looked through one of the glass panels in the front door and an annoyed exclamation burst from her.

'What's up?' the red head asked.

'There're lawmen coming without Mick needing to send them!' Belle replied.

'It was that bunch back there's was trying to slicker *you*,' Calamity pointed out, gazing through the second panel. A sergeant and two patrolmen, wearing the uniform of the

Topeka Police Department, were approaching along the path in a buckboard. 'Not tuther way 'round – for *once*.'

'A body would think I go around slickering folks all the time, way you talk,' the lady outlaw protested, amused by the way the comment had ended and replying in kind, despite having a better appreciation of how the situation had changed due to the unexpected arrival of the peace officers. 'But I don't want to be asked to explain *our* part in it, especially with the marked cards and forged money back there.'

'Nor me, comes to that!' Calamity conceded.

'Could you get away without being seen if you went through those French windows you busted?' Belle asked.

'I've snuck by Injuns when needed and'm still wearing my hair!'[10]

'Go to it then!'

'How about *you*?'

'I've talked my way by lawmen when needed and never wound up making hair bridles in a jail,' Belle replied, not displeased by her friend's concern for her welfare and referring to a task frequently carried out by prisoners in Western penitentiaries. 'Get going and leave me do it again!'

Accepting the lady outlaw was far more experienced than herself in such matters, Calamity did as she was instructed. Hurrying through the dining-room, where a couple of the feminists were beginning to stir – although, she noticed with relief, neither had recovered sufficiently to be able to do anything which might attract the attention of the peace officers – she looked out of the French windows cautiously and jerked back her head almost immediately. It seemed that getting away would not be as simple as she had envisaged. The buckboard was halted in front of the main entrance and, although she felt sure that she had not been seen, the sergeant was pointing in her direction. Wondering if he had noticed the damaged door despite the drapes having fallen back into place after she went through, or seen her whip hanging from the upstairs balcony, she turned and

10. One occasion is described in: TROUBLE TRAIL.

darted back across the room. However, before she could go into the entrance hall, she saw the lady outlaw was opening the front door and stopped in her tracks to listen.

'Th—Thank *heavens* you've come, officers!' Belle gasped, adopting a Mid-West accent which seemed to be quavering with alarm and fear.

'What's up, lady!' a deep masculine voice demanded from outside the building.

Deciding the lady outlaw had seen what was happening and was trying to create a diversion which would prevent a man being sent to investigate whatever had attracted the attention of the sergeant, Calamity swung around. Running to the French windows and easing between the drapes, a glance informed her that both patrolmen were following the sergeant through the front door. Going outside, she grabbed the handle of her whip and shook it free. Crossing the porch, with the lash trailing behind her like a long tail, she vaulted the balustrade and darted silently to the nearest bushes. Crouching in concealment, coiling the lash, she turned her attention to the front door and watched how Belle was coping with the unanticipated development.

'I—In there!' the lady outlaw gasped, concealing her relief at the way her appearance was preventing the patrolman being sent to the French windows.

'What's in there?' the sergeant inquired, as he and his companions gazed across the entrance hall instead of behind them.

'I—I was asked to come here to attend a meeting of the Women's Rights Movement,' Belle explained in a breathless fashion, watching the red head taking cover without being detected. 'B—But they tried to get me into a game of poker and—and—!'

'Yes, ma'am?' the sergeant prompted, darting a glance at the patrolmen.

'One of them was caught using marked cards by the others,' Belle obliged. 'Th—Then a f—fight started – a *real* one, not just shouting and arguing—and—and I was so *afraid.* In fact, one of them *attacked* me and to—tore my b—blouse.'

'Take it easy, ma'am!' the sergeant said and his companions mumbled just as sympathetically. 'You're safe *now.* We're here and'll 'tend to them. From what you say, it looks like that letter we got saying them Women's women bunch're running a crooked poker game here's right. Come back in and sit dow—!'[11]

'I—I don't want to go into that room again!' the lady outlaw interrupted, speaking the complete truth even though not for the reason which the three peace officers were drawing. 'In fact, I want to get out of this house. I—I'm staying next door with my Uncle Winston, that's *Senator Dillwater* you know, and won't feel *safe* until I'm back there.'

'I'll come with you, ma'am,' the taller of the patrolmen offered and the other repeated the suggestion at almost the same moment.

'Y—You'll *all* be needed to deal with *them,*' Belle replied, pointing behind her. 'I'll go through the gate in the garden wall as I did when I came here and wait for you there. I'm *sure* Uncle Winston will want to thank you for coming just in time.'

'It'd be best if you wait here, ma'am,' the sergeant suggested, wanting to be sure it was he and not one of his subordinates received whatever praise was forthcoming for looking after Senator Winston Dillwater's niece. 'We'll 'tend to those gals and then *I'll* go with you.'

'W—Whatever you say,' Belle assented, going to flop rather than just sit on a chair by the hall stand. 'Go and do your duty, gentlemen, and I'm sure my uncle will be most grateful when I tell him what you've done.'

'They're all down and out, serge,' the taller of the patrolmen announced, having strode to the door of the

11. Belle Starr subsequently learned the authorities were informed anonymously by a gang of card sharps who were annoyed about what they regarded as interlopers operating in their territory.

dining-room. The feminists had caused the Police Department a great deal of trouble during the election campaign and a note of satisfaction came into his voice as he continued, 'Why don't we go fetch some buckets of water from the kitchen and douse 'em to bring 'em 'round?'

'Do you think that is *wise*, sergeant?' Belle inquired. 'From what Uncle Winston has told me about the owner of this house, he won't take it kindly that his carpet was ruined by policemen, no mattter how good your reason.'

'The lady's right about that, serge,' the second patrolman supported, knowing the owner was a lawyer whose political aspirations made him hostile to peace officers. 'he's *allus* against us.'

'You don't need to tell me *that*,' the sergeant asserted. 'Leave 'em to come 'round their own way. Don't even touch 'em, or they're likely to claim you was mauling their bodies all promiscuous and lewd, same's their kind's been doing every time we've had to fetch 'em away from where they was causing trouble. Let's take a look at the cards and we can talk to them when they've come 'round on their own.'

'You sure you'll be all right, ma'am?' the shorter patrolman inquired solicitously.

'Yes,' Belle confirmed. 'I'll stay here until you've finished and I feel it would be advisable for you all to be together so that you can serve as witnesses to one another's actions if those *dreadful* women try to accuse you of misbehaving. In fact, if they do, call me in and I'll give you my support.'

'That's real good of you, ma'am,' the sergeant declared. 'Come on, boys. Let's go take a look.'

From her place of concealment behind the bushes, being able to see and hear everything through the open front door, Calamity was impressed and amused by the performance of the lady outlaw. It was quite a feat for one of her height and far from unnoticeable physical attributes to contrive to look small and helpless in a fashion which aroused the protective instincts of all three burly peace officers and persuaded them to do as she required. She had achieved her purpose and, after the trio entered the dining- room, she emerged to hurry along the path.

* * *

'Far be it for me to say I told you so,' Belle Starr commented, having slid down the rope supplied by the hotel as a means of escape in case of fire. 'But I told you there'd be time for me to come here and pick up all my belongings.'

'And I'll bet I *never* hear the last of it,' Calamity Jane replied, holding the carpetbag which had been dropped from the window by the lady outlaw. 'Let's get going.'

Having seen the policemen coming from the other direction and turning through the gates, the driver had brought his hackney cab from where he was waiting further along the street. Leaving the vehicle out of sight, he had kept watch along the path and, because of the debt of gratitude he owed to Dobey Killem and the liking he had formed for Calamity Jane, he had been ready to do whatever he could to help her and her companion escape should this prove necessary. They had got away without any need for intervention on his part and, once they were aboard, he had driven off at a speed suggestive of urgency, but not sufficiently fast to arouse suspicion.

On the way to the hotel, Belle had done what she could to make herself presentable for going inside. Using a towel from the bag she had given to the red head when explaining her plan for dealing with the feminists, she had dried her face and torso. Then, while Calamity was doing the same with a clean shirt, she had extracted and changed into a blouse similar to the one damaged in the fighting. Asked about her plans now the situation had changed so drastically, she had stated her belief that there would be sufficient time before the suspicions of the sergeant were directed her way for her to collect her property and make good her escape.

Reverting to being 'Betty Hardin' and behaving in a flustered and embarrassed manner while retrieving the jewellery she had left in the safe, Belle had informed the desk clerk that she did not wish to be disturbed by Mary Abbott or any other member of the Women's Rights Movement. Suspecting their sexual proclivities, he had drawn the conclusion she sought to produce and assumed the insistence stemmed from them having tried to force their attentions upon her. Having locked and bolted the door of her room, she had packed the carpetbag. Dropping it to where Calamity was waiting in the alley, she had made her descent without difficulty or being seen by anybody else.

'As if *I'd* boast about *anything*,' Belle said, as she and Calamity set off to where the driver was waiting with his hackney cab. 'But I *did* tell you how Abbott and her kind hate peace officers near as much as they hate us Southrons and wouldn't be wanting to admit to *men*– especially *lawmen* – how a Southron girl took them the way I did. Besides which, even when he found out that I'd gone instead of staying, I reckon the sergeant'd be even more willing to reckon it was them and not Senator Dillwater's niece who brought the forged cash and marked cards into the game.'

'He's going to be riled as a stick-teased rattler when he finds out you're not kin to the Senator,' Calamity guessed.

'Why sure,' the lady outlaw agreed. 'Only, by the time either he or any other of the local law comes looking for 'Betty Hardin', she'll be long gone. And I reckon it would be better if you're not around either, Calam.'

'Something told me's I'd likely wind up that way, the company I've been keeping,' the red head replied, confident that her friend could elude any pursuit given so much of a start. Having anticipated the contingency, she had made arrangements for her safety with the approval of Dobey Killem. 'So I've got my gear packed and a hoss waiting. Should anybody go 'round the outfit and ask, they'll get told I lit out at sundown to see what the trail end towns have to offer, 'cause Topeka's been too danged quiet for me. Which it was afore our trails crossed and'd get that way again once you've gone.'[12]

12. As Belle Starr expected, when the feminists recovered, the antagonism their kind had for everybody connected with the enforcement of law and order had caused them to refuse to answer any of the questions put by the sergeant. Being experienced in such things, he sent the taller patrolman to fetch one of his superiors to deal with the situation. Confronted by a senior member of the Topeka Police Department and a United States Marshal who accompanied him with the evidence that cheating had taken place and the presence of a substantial sum of counterfeit money, they finally claimed they were tricked into playing poker by 'Betty Hardin' and it was she who brought the marked cards and the forged bills into the game. Without mentioning Calamity Jane, they asserted she had called in half a dozen female associates to attack them when they became suspicious. By the time it was ascertained that Senator Dillwater did not have a niece paying a visit and men were dispatched to check up on 'Betty Hardin', Belle Starr had returned to the home of her associate and was back in the disguise of the nun. Receiving her promissory note on the day after the game, Ruby Wakefield had expressed the intention of handing the feminists over to the police. However, she accepted the warning from the 'Mother Superior' that to do so would cause the matter to be made public and bring embarrassment to herself and her family and went home without saying anything.

12a. Although they had not been brought to trial, Mary Abbott and her group feared they would be as a result of the complaints they believed would be lodged when their victims received the promissory notes. Therefore, they fled to the East and, scattering, were never again involved in the feminist campaign. Although the authorities suspected Belle Starr had been 'Betty Hardin', it was considered she had done the community a service by getting rid of them and there was no attempt made to prove her implication.

APPENDIX ONE

Unlike her partner, Deputy Sheriff Bradford 'Brad' Counter, Woman Deputy Alice Fayde entered the Rockabye County Sheriff's Office by conventional means. Prior to the appointment, she had served seven years on the Gusher City Police Department's Bureau Of Women Officers, rising through the ranks from walking a beat as a uniformed patrolwoman to becoming a sergeant in the Detective Bureau. She had worked in such diverse Divisions as Evans Park – the slum area known as the 'Bad Bit' – and high-rent Upton Heights. She had also spent time in various specialist Squads, such as Traffic, Juvenile and Narcotics. All of which had combined to give her a very thorough knowledge of law enforcement duties. Furthermore, she had become an expert shot with a handgun and skilled at unarmed combat. As a deputy, she had a rank equivalent to a lieutenant in the G.C.P.D.'s Patrol Bureau, or a detective sergeant.

In addition to their other duties, the Sheriff's Office were responsible for the investigation throughout the whole of Rockabye County of homicide and twenty-two other legal infractions – such as arson, wife-beating, bigamy, assault and train wrecking – which might end in murder. The idea behind handling the subsidiary crimes was so that, if death should result through their commission, the officers in charge would already have knowledge of the facts leading up to it.

The Sheriff's Office based in the Gusher City Department Of Public Safety Building worked a two-watch rota. The Day Watch commenced at eight in the morning and ended at four in the afternoon, with the Night Watch continuing from four until midnight. If deputies were required between midnight and eight in the morning, the G.C.P.D.'s permanently manned 'Business Office' of the Bureau of Communications would call them from their homes.

The jurisdictional authority of a town marshal in the Old West – sometimes known as the 'constable' in smaller towns – or modern police department was restricted to the municipality by whom they were hired and the sheriff's office within the boundaries of its county. As was suggested by the title of the latter, Arizona and Texas Rangers and State Police were restricted to their specific States. The Texas Rangers and their contemporaries in Arizona were generally expected to wait until invited by county or municipal agencies before being able to participate in an investigation.[1] United States marshals and deputy marshals, the Federal Bureau of Investigation and the 'bomber boys' of the Inland Revenue Service's Tobacco and Alcohol Tax Division had country wide jurisdiction. However, the first three were responsible only for handling 'Federal' crimes and the latter was restricted to dealing with legal infractions involving the production, transportation and sale of tobacco products and alcoholic beverages.

1. *During the Prohibition era, Company 'Z' of the Texas Rangers had authorization from the Governor and State Attorney General to instigate investigations of a special nature without awaiting invitation by the local law enforcement agencies. See:* APPENDIX TWO.

2. *Information about a similar arrangement granted to the Arizona Rangers is given in the* WACO *series.*

APPENDIX TWO

In every democracy, the laws framed for the protection of the innocent have loopholes which can be exploited for the benefit of the undeniably guilty – and frequently are!

Although accepting that such a state of affairs must exist in a free society, the serving Governor of Texas grew very concerned over the ever increasing wave of lawlessness which had followed in the wake of the well meant – albeit unpopular, ill advised and difficult to enforce – ratification of the so called 'Volstead Act'.[1] He concluded that only unconventional methods could cope with malefactors who slipped through the meshes of the legal system. Ordinary peace officers, being severely restricted by Federal, State, county and municipal regulations, were unable to take the necessary action in circumstances of this nature.

While pondering upon the problem, the Governor met three prominent European criminologists who were touring the United States and giving a series of lectures on

1. 'Volstead Act', the colloquial name for the Eighteenth (Prohibition) Amendment to the Constitution on the United States of America. This defined intoxicating liquors as those containing more than one half of one percent alcohol and made illegal the manufacture, transportation and sale of such liquors for beverage purposes. Introduced by Representative Andrew J. Volstead of Minnesota, the act was ratified – over the veto of President Woodrow Wilson – on October the 18th, 1919. By the time it was repealed in 1933, it had inadvertantly helped finance and pave the way for the rise of 'organized crime'.

this subject to the heads of major law enforcement agencies. Acting upon the unconventional suggestions of George Manfred, Leon Gonzales and Raymond Poiccart,[2] he had instructed the State Attorney General to select a special group of Texas Rangers who would form – without any mention of it being made public – a new Company given the identifying letter 'Z' and put under the command of Major Benson Tragg. Every man was picked for his courage, skill with weapons and at bare handed combat, integrity, specialized knowledge and devotion to the cause of justice. Their purpose was to deal with such criminals as could not be touched by conventional methods, even if the means they employed to do so might be considered as stepping beyond the legal boundaries of the law.[3]

Having met members of Company 'Z' while they were engaged in trapping a crooked financier who could not be extradited from Mexico, Rita Yarborough, who was trying to take revenge upon him for causing the death of her parents, was made an 'official unofficial' member of the

2. George Manfred, Leon Gonzales and Raymond Poiccart were the surviving members of the 'Four Just Men' crime fighting organization, the fourth having been killed before their first recorded adventure was published. Although none of the following volumes cover their lecture tour of the United States, see chronologically: THE FOUR JUST MEN, THE COUNCIL OF JUSTICE, THE LAW OF THE FOUR JUST MEN, AGAIN THE THREE *and* THE THREE JUST MEN, *by Edgar Wallace.*

3. The Texas Rangers were to all practical intents and purposes abolished – their functions being taken over by the more prosaic Department Of Public Safety at Austin and the Highway Patrol – on October the 17th, 1935. This was almost one hundred years to the day after their formation. Although their first purpose was to act as militia, or what in present day terms would be called a 'paramilitary' organization, to help fend off marauding Indians, they became increasingly responsible for supporting the local authorities in the enforcement of law and order.

group.[4] She proved herself very useful, particularly when there was a need to deal with other women in the course of Company 'Z's' specialized type of duties.[5]

4. *Told in:* RAPIDO CLINT.

4a. *The first 'lone hand' assignment carried out by Rita Yarborough is described in:* Part Two, 'Behind A Locked And Bolted Door', MORE J.T.'S LADIES.

5. *An example of how Rita Yarborough dealt with another woman in the course of an assignment is given in:* THE RETURN OF RAPIDO CLINT AND MR. J.G. REEDER.

APPENDIX THREE

Deserted by her husband, Charlotte Canary decided the best way she could ensure a safe future for her children was to leave them in a convent at St. Louis and head West to seek her fortune.[1] However, there had been far too much of her lively and reckless spirit in her eldest daughter, Martha Jane, for the scheme to be successful. Rebelling against the strict life imposed by the nuns, the girl celebrated her fifteenth birthday by running away. Hiding in one of Cecil 'Dobey' Killem's freight wagons, she had been carried some twelve miles from the city before being discovered. She might have been sent back to the convent, but the cook was found too drunk to work. One of the things which she had learned from the nuns was good, plain cooking and the meal she prepared was so satisfactory she had support from the drivers in persuading Killem to take her to Wichita, Kansas, where she claimed she had an aunt who would give her a home.

During the outfit's roundabout route to its destination, raiding Sioux warriors who wiped out two other outfits failed to locate them. What was more, all the goods they were transporting were sold at a good profit and Killem was given a lucrative contract to deliver supplies further West, so the crew received a bonus. Learning the aunt was a figment of the girl's imagination and having come to consider her as a good luck charm, the drivers had prevailed

1. Some information about the subsequent career of Charlotte Canary is given in: Part One, 'Better Than Calamity', TROUBLED RANGE *and, supplying greater detail, its two 'expansions';* THE HIDE AND HORN SALOON *and* CUT ONE, THEY ALL BLEED.

upon their employer to let her stay with them. Not that he, having taken a liking to her for her spunk and cheerful disposition, had taken much persuading.

At first, the girl helped the cook and, wearing masculine attire for convenience, carried out other menial duties. She soon graduated to driving and, learning fast, in a short while there was little she could not do in that line of work. Not only could she harness and drive the six-horse team of a Conestoga wagon, she carried out its maintenance and their care to Killem's exacting requirements. She was taught how to use a long lashed bull whip as an inducement to equestrian activity, or as a most effective weapon, to handle firearms with some skill and generally take care of herself on the open ranges west of the Mississippi River. Nor did her self reliance end there. Visiting saloons with the other members of the crew, she was frequently called upon to defend herself against the objections of the female denizens who resented her trespassing on their domain. Although the lady outlaw, Belle Starr, *q.v.* held her to a hard fought draw when they first met,[2] leading a much more active and healthy life than the saloon-girls, she was only beaten once.[3]

Courageous, loyal to anybody who won her friendship, happy go lucky and so generous she deliberately lost her share of a saloon she had inherited jointly with professional gambler, Frank Derringer,[4] the girl had a penchant for becoming involved in dangerous and precarious situations.

2. *The first meeting between Calamity Jane and the lady outlaw is recorded in:* Part One, 'The Bounty On Belle Starr's Scalp', THE WILDCATS *and, with added information, its 'expansion',* CALAMITY, MARK AND BELLE.

3. *Details of the one defeat are given in the titles referred to in:* Footnote One.

4. *Told in:* COLD DECK, HOT LEAD

4a. *Further details of the career of the professional gambler, Frank Derringer, are to be found in:* QUIET TOWN; THE MAKING OF A LAWMAN; THE TROUBLE BUSTERS; DECISION FOR DUSTY FOG; DIAMONDS, EMERALDS, CARDS AND COLTS *and* THE GENTLE GIANT.

Visiting New Orleans, she acted as decoy to bring the Strangler – a notorious mass murderer of young 'ladies of the evening' – to justice.[5] While on a delivery of supplies to an Army post further West, she fought with three women, including a professional female bare-knuckle boxer, then helped rescue a cavalry officer captured by Indians.[6] In Texas, she played a part in wiping out a wave of cattle stealing which was threatening to cause a range war.[7] What started as an innocent and peaceful journey on a stagecoach ended with her being compelled to take over as driver and help capture the outlaws who robbed it.[8] Going to visit a ranch left to her by her father, accompanied by the Ysabel Kid, she was nearly killed when a rival claimant had her fastened to a log which was being sent through a circular saw.[9] Accompanying Belle 'the Rebel Spy' Boyd, *q.v.* and Captain Patrick 'the Remittance Kid' Reeder,[10] she played a major part in averting an Indian uprising in Canada. During a big game hunt with a visiting British sportsman and his sister, she was kidnapped.[11].

Among her friends, she counted the members of the

5. *Told in:* THE BULL WHIP BREED.

6. *Told in:* TROUBLE TRAIL.

7. *Told in:* THE COW THIEVES.

8. *Told in:* CALAMITY SPELLS TROUBLE.

9. *Told in:* WHITE STALLION, RED MARE.

10. *Told in:* THE WHIP AND THE WAR LANCE.

10a. *The researches of Phillip Jose Farmer,* q.v., *have established that Captain Patrick Reeder (later Major General Sir, K.C.B, V.C., D.S.O., M.C. and Bar) was the uncle of the celebrated British detective, Mr. Jeremiah Golden Reeder, whose biography appears in:* ROOM 13, THE MIND OF MR. J.G. REEDER, RED ACES, MR. J.G. REEDER RETURNS *and* TERROR KEEP, *by Edgar Wallace.*

10b. *Mr. Jeremiah Golden Reeder's organization play a prominent part in the events we recorded as:* 'CAP' FOG, TEXAS RANGER, MEET MR. J.G. REEDER *and* THE RETURN OF RAPIDO CLINT AND MR. J.G. REEDER.

11. *Told in:* THE BIG HUNT.

OD Connected ranch's floating outfit, being on particularly good terms with Mark Counter.[12] On one memorable occasion, although there was no ceremony in church and the marriage was most certainly *not* consummated, she posed as the wife of Captain Dustine Marsden 'Dusty' Fog, in a scheme to trap a gang of land grabbers.[13] Other close acquaintances were James Butler 'Wild Bill' Hickok and his wife, Agnes,[14] and she captured his murderer on the day he was killed.[15]

Because of her penchant for finding so much trouble and getting involved in brawls, the girl soon acquired the sobriquet by which she became famous throughout the West and beyond.

People called her 'Calamity Jane'!

THE END

12. Details of the association between Calamity Jane and Mark Counter are recorded in various volumes of the Floating Outfit *series, which – in addition to the* Civil War *series – also records the adventures of Captain Dustine Edward Marsden 'Dusty' Fog and the Ysabel Kid.*

13. Told in: Part Two, 'A Wife For Dusty Fog', THE SMALL TEXAN.

14. One meeting between Calamity Jane and Agnes Hickok is described in: Part Six, 'Mrs. Wild Bill', J.T.'S LADIES.

15. Told in: Part Seven, 'Deadwood, August 2nd, 1876', J.T.'S HUNDREDTH.

15a. James Butler 'Wild Bill' Hickok makes 'guest' appearances in: Part One, The Scout, UNDER THE STARS AND BARS *and* Part Six, 'Eggars' Try', THE TOWN TAMERS.